MA

D0438591

Indelible Acts

Indelible Acts

Stories

A. L. KENNEDY

Alfred A. Knopf   New York   2003

THIS IS A BORZOI BOOK
PUBLISHED BY ALFRED A. KNOPF

Copyright 2002 by A. L. Kennedy

www.aaknopf.com

Originally published in Great Britain by Jonathan Cape,
Random House UK, London, in 2002.

Library of Congress Cataloging-in-Publication Data
Kennedy, A. L.
Indelible acts : a collection of stories / by A. L. Kennedy.—1st ed.
p.   cm.
ISBN 1-4000-4055-8
1. Love stories, English. 2. Loss (Psychology)—Fiction.
3. Adultery—Fiction. I. Title.
PR6061.E5952 I54 2003
823'.914—DC21   2002030179

Manufactured in the United States of America
First American Edition

Mo rùn geal òg

Contents

Indelible Acts

Spared

Things could go wrong with one letter, he knew that now. Just one.

"Actually, I moved here ten years ago."

He had found it so terribly, pleasantly effortless to say, "Actually, I moved here ten years ago."

There had only been a little thickness about the *m*, a tiny falter there that might have suggested a stammer, or a moment's pause to let him total up those years. Nobody listening, surely, would have guessed his intended sentence had been, "Actually, I'm married." In the course of one consonant everything had changed.

He'd been standing in the cheese queue. His bright idea: to visit the cheese shop, the specialist. Even though such places annoyed him and made him think there was too much money in the world being spent in far too many stupid ways, he had gone to the purveyors of nothing but cheese and things cheese-related to buy something nice for Christmas, a treat. Of course, thirty other people had been taken with the same idea and were lined right through and out of the shop and then along the pavement, all variously huddled and leaning away from the intermittent press of sleety rain. There was an awning, but it didn't help. And, at that point, he should simply have gone home, but for no particular reason, he did not.

Instead, he stood and turned up his collar and peered, like everyone else, into the cheese shop window where the cheesemongers, busy and vaguely smug, trotted about in white wellingtons, white jackets, white hats. The facts that he personally didn't much like cheese, that his gloves were back, safe and warm, in the car, and that any wait here now would be quite ludicrously dismal—none of these disturbed him. On the contrary, they seemed perversely satisfying: a rare chance to perform an unpleasant task that was wholly of his own choosing.

His satisfaction had, quite reasonably, produced a happy kind of pressure in his chest which had caused him to turn and say, really to no one, "They look like dentists, don't they?" and then to smile.

"Yes, dentists. Or maybe vets. Cheese vets."

And he'd been mildly aware of a girl in the shop window smoothly drawing down a wire and opening up the white heart of something or other with one slice, but mainly there'd been this woman standing behind him in the queue, this woman he had never met, and then there'd been this thought which had said very softly but unmistakably, *My God, she has a wonderful voice.* This thought which had seemed just as confident and hungry as he'd always meant and never quite managed to be.

Although, truthfully, what it said wasn't really right—she had a perfect voice.

He could almost hear her now, if he concentrated: lying awake—as usual awake—and grinning like a night light, because he could imagine the flavour of her *maybe* and her *yes*.

His right arm, the one that was furthest from Karen in their bed, the one that was his least matrimonial arm, was crooked up to let his wrist settle in nicely under his head and make him, at least, a comfortable insomniac. He was trying to breathe as if he wasn't conscious, wasn't turning helplessly inside his kicking mind, wasn't opening and closing his eyes between one type of blank and another to see which was best as a background for the image of a woman who wasn't Karen, who wasn't in any way his wife.

Dark coat, mainly dark with water, but also sensible and warm—his mind now slipped away to thoughts of silky linings, but he pulled it back—a golden-coloured scarf that covered up her chin—he did like that—and then one of those horrible hill-walker's fleecy hats which, in this case, looked fantastic because it was hers, she was wearing it.

He had been immediately, impossibly, mortally charmed. The truth of this made a brief swell in his breathing, followed by a sigh.

"Greg, *please*." By which Karen didn't mean, "Greg, *please* torment me with your luscious manhood now and for the rest of the night until I speak in tongues." She meant—half asleep, but still determined, she always was determined—"Greg, *please* either fall asleep now or go to the spare room and give me peace, because I've got to get up for work tomorrow morning, just as early as you do."

So, like a dutiful and undisturbing partner, he slid out of bed on to one braced arm, one knee, and then staggered softly up into a standing position and took himself away. This had happened before the cheese queue, this type of midnight banishment: Greg hadn't really slept well in months. The muffling of the pillow at his ears could very easily make him picture coffins and drowsiness often produced a sensation of morbid, jerked descent, as if into a curiously sticky grave. He suffered from nocturnal sweats.

By the time he had joked to Karen over breakfast that fixing up a variation on a Victorian casket alarm might keep him calmer, she hadn't found his difficulties funny. He had tried, although he was extremely tired, to be more playful, to expand the idea, suggesting that he really should tie one finger with thread in the hope that his subconscious might believe itself safely connected to the brand of handy little bell designed, in a more cautious age, to prevent premature burial.

"You should try the pills again—break the cycle."

"The pills made me sleep in the daytime. I can't keep being discovered in the office with my head on the desk, people will end up thinking I have a life." This said in a self-deprecating and not vicious way, but all the same.

"You *do* have a life. It just seems incompatible with mine." *This* said in a way that was a little light-hearted, but with eyes that fixed him for a threatening moment before she went to turn over the toast. "We should get a toaster."

"I'll get one."

"You'll forget, you always forget."

"I'll get one. Tomorrow: I can't today."

"Mm hm."

Greg loathed the way she did that; closing everything off with her favourite passive/aggressive little noise, the agreement that didn't agree—*Mm hm.*

"Mm hm."

In other times, though, in other places, it was a good sound to make. In that other time, that other place, it had been the best. "Mm hm. They could be vets, couldn't, they . . . Yes."

He settled his limbs out in the chill of the spare bed and recalled the horrifying pause when the conversation might have faltered, stopped, and left him to the queue, let his head go sliding under, back into the fetid sump that held his nights and days. He'd known, in a way that made his ears ache, that he hated his shoes, his not waterproof shoes, and that his latest haircut had

been shoddy and would look especially dreadful when it was wet and that naked drips of rain were clinging just exactly where they shouldn't on his face: like unwanted ear-rings, tears, snot: but he'd kept himself steady, he'd raised his chin—broken his very personal, gloomy surface—and stolen a breath. And, blinking into her face, he'd understood that this whole situation might possibly, conceivably, turn out fine. He might come to be as he'd like to be, without breakages or loss, because she was smiling, smiling only at him.

Greg's hands scrambled for his pockets and a fraying tissue that rapidly transformed itself into a greyish wad, "Christ, what a day," and he mopped his face while praying sincerely that he wouldn't sound so cretinous the next time he opened his mouth.

"Yes, but it'll be worth it."

And he did realise she was talking about the cheese, saying simply that the bloody cheese would be worth the wait, but still he felt himself swallow, needed to hold one hand in the other and couldn't help stumbling back with, "Yes. It will. I hope. No, it will. Naturally. Yes" before coughing out a remarkably ugly and—in God's name—unmistakably equine, laugh.

"I don't suppose any of us come here normally—it's just Christmas, isn't it?"

So is she celebrating Christmas for herself, or for somebody else who is with her, who is allowed to touch her face?

"It can't be absolutely *just* Christmas . . ." *Don't contradict her—what the fuck are you doing?* "I mean, I mean . . ." *Do you* **want** *her to be pissed off?* "They must get *some* customers, sometimes—they stay open . . ." *Oh, that was scintillating, wasn't it? Well fucking done.*

"Maybe they're only a front for the CIA."

God, thank you, God. "Now that you mention it, I did see them shoot this shoplifter once . . ."

"Execution-style with a silenced gun?"

"Absolutely. Extremely professional."

"Oh, well then, that's that. Definitely CIA. Or MI5."

I want to lick her. Now. The rain from her eyes. Just to lick. "Do you think we should still let them have our money?"

"Yes. But only if they give us cheese."

They were properly established then, talking: about the absurdities of Christmas, about tropical holidays neither of them would take, about the concept of cheese which—if you thought of it—was a strange one.

"I mean—cheese—you couldn't have come up with that by accident." He felt warmer, he felt taller, he felt fate snuggling round him with a good, good plan. "Cheese." His tongue moved in his mouth especially deftly, as if each word were more than usually intended. "But who would have thought to try and make it—who would have known *how?*"

"I know, it's like bread dough with yeast, or meringues—especially meringues. Who on earth could have guessed *that* would happen to an egg white if you pummelled it enough?"

"I think the correct term is *beat*." While he thought, "But pummel would do, I'm sure," he could really do nothing *but* think, "There must have been a Lost Meringue Age"; that egg white looked so much like spunk, *was* so much like spunk.

Spunk. There was nowhere his mind wasn't willing to go and he was so happy to follow it nearly scared him.

I wonder what she sounds like when she comes.

"The Meringue Age." She patted his forearm quickly, approvingly. "Of course, the Lost Meringue Age. An era of peace and random food experiments."

I will know what she sounds like when she comes. I will be there and I will hear her and I will see. I have to.

But no harm done, only thinking.

His eyelids had closed and he couldn't quite coax them back

apart. *Under her knee, in that curve, there would be sweat. And in between—*

"Your accent, by the way . . . If you don't mind my asking, where are you from?"

Greg finally eased his eyes open: peeled up a muzzled guess at the shape of her thighs, of her arse, laid naked for his hand: and he saw her face. She met his gaze, seemed to take it from him whole, while he tried to organise a sentence, "Oh, I . . . My accent? Well, I used to live in England."

"Ah, English—as I suspected. And you haven't been here long?"

A brief knot of conscience and impatience lashed open at the base of his brain and, before he could stop himself, he'd told her, "Actually, I *moved* here ten years ago," which wasn't exactly a lie.

After which, there had been no stopping, no space in his will for even a pause. By the time they'd made it inside the shop, he'd known it was safe to play, make a little rehearsal, and pretend that he was shopping with a girlfriend, a sexual partner, a woman who would never look revolted if he asked her to suck his cock, who would never clatter him with her molars in little bounces of mute revenge and then swallow what he surrendered as if it were only cruel and unusual and not a part of him.

Shopping with Karen was hardly exciting, either: it was like shopping with himself only slower and more expensive. It was one of the things they did together which had, at no time, ever been any fun. That day in the queue had been different, though, that day when he'd gone shopping with somebody new.

"This is silly."

"What is?" She'd been almost, almost leaning against him while the cheesemonger cut two pieces each of their choices— one to keep and one to swap, which was what they'd decided. "What's silly?"

Greg had dipped his head and spoken close, close as a kiss beside her ear, because this was appropriate under the circumstances and because he'd hoped that she might like it. "That we've talked for ages—about half an hour—and now we're buying cheese together . . ."

"Which is a very personal thing." She was joking and not joking—he liked that. He loved that.

This is the way you seduce someone, isn't it. Who could have guessed I'd remember how. And this is the time to do it, maybe the last chance to try.

"Yes. Extremely personal." And now Greg wasn't joking at all. "But we don't know each other's names. That can't be right." He angled near again, made this soft, "Can it?"

"Amanda."

"Really? That's great." Because he'd been rushed by the lunatic fear that she might be called Karen, or something like Karen. "Wonderful." Not that anything *was* like Karen.

"Why?"

"Oh . . . I don't know—it suits you. That kind of idea. I'm Greg." *Say my name.* "So now we know each other, that's good." *Say my name.*

"Greg. OK. Great."

Say my name when I'm in you and I probably will weep.

Amanda was waiting for a quarter pound of olives—he didn't like olives, but she was free to—when he asked her, "Look, I don't know your phone number, either, do I?" Which was speeding the process more than he ought, but he'd have to go home soon: he was practically late now, Saturday's dinner already suppurating in the microwave, no doubt. "It's just that I would like to take you and have a coffee—"

"To take me *and* have a coffee?"

"Well . . ." He watched her mouth, "Yes. I like coffee. Only

I can't do it now, I have to . . . go out tonight with . . . no one."
Good mouth. Wonderful mouth. "But I have to . . . go out and
so . . . If I had your number, I could phone. It's the gentleman
who phones, isn't? I have got that right?"

Greg hadn't intended this to make her laugh, but believed it
to be a splendid thing when she did. "The *gentleman*? So you're
a gentleman?"

He checked her eyes. "At times."

She paused for precisely long enough to please him very
much. "OK."

Amanda had offered a pen but no paper and all of the cheese
wrappings, they'd discovered, were greased and wouldn't take
ink, so he'd rolled up his sleeve, delighted, and let her write her
number on the inside of his wrist.

He'd kept the secret on him all that evening: had taken it,
and never mind the risk, with him into bed. The tickle of her nib
had set his skin ringing for hours until he had to pad off, volun-
tarily, into the other room and stretch out on top of the covers,
stiffer than he'd been in years. And for almost fifteen minutes
he'd only tensed, spread like a starfish, and concentrated on
reclaiming the scent of her hair. Then, locked silently in the bathroom, he'd come twice: the first time through a kind of wrench-
ing haze, the second more melancholy, empty. By the time he'd
got back and into bed, he'd been completely lonely. He'd dreamed
briefly of an undefined apocalypse and gasped back awake with
the idea of kissing her throat.

Greg couldn't be here now without a trace of that night
pressing through, as if she'd really joined him somehow and this
had become their bed. As if his loneliness had been sweated into
fragments in this room and not another.

"I want to see everything."

"What?"

After he'd had coffee with Amanda, and then after they'd met for lunch, he'd chiselled out one complete evening, to have for his own. They'd eaten dinner in Amanda's flat, his imagination ceaselessly bolting and clambering, and then she'd gone through to the kitchen to fetch their dessert.

"I said I want to see everything."

He'd been rolling an olive gently between his forefinger and thumb, hoping that if he made the bloody thing seem vaguely horny he might fancy eating it. He'd only been able to kiss Amanda once, a little, since he'd arrived and perhaps this was all there would be now: perhaps women, once they knew him, didn't find him attractive, perhaps he'd got too old: he couldn't tell and it was all just worrying. But this was when she'd called, "I don't want us to put the lights out." She appeared in the doorway and paused, holding out two plates of lemon cake. "I don't want us to close our eyes, or run and hide under the duvet, as if it wasn't really happening. I want to see everything."

"Oh." He would have swallowed, but had no spit. And he didn't want any cake.

"Was that the wrong way to say it? I didn't mean to be—"

"I want to see everything, too." This not the kind of stuff that he would ordinarily admit. "I've wanted to . . ." Perhaps because there was, ordinarily, no point.

"You've wanted to what?" She put the plates down on the table as he turned in his chair to face her. He watched her walk towards him, only halting when her knees were touching his. "I don't mind. I don't *think* I'll mind—what?"

With the crook of one finger he stroked her stomach through her blouse, easing down, aware of a nice, taut heat, "I just wasn't sure . . ." and he understood why she hadn't touched him at all this evening, "I didn't know how to put it . . ." She'd known that if she started she wouldn't stop. He hoped that was it. Or maybe she'd known that, if she started, *he* wouldn't stop.

"You wouldn't be offended if I told you that I wanted to fuck you the first time we met." She laced both her hands at the back of his head while he looked up and his mouth made declarations he'd never expected, "Now that . . . we've properly introduced ourselves and I like you and I think I love you, probably, I do want to make love to you, but I still want to fuck you. I want both."

Amanda nuzzled the top of his head. "All right."

"You mean that's all right?" He was whispering, in case he made this go away.

"That's what I said. Yes. That's all right. Do you want your cake first?"

"No, I don't. I really don't, definitely. No. I do not."

"You don't like lemon cake?"

"Amanda, *please.*"

They didn't have long enough, really, not as long as he'd have liked.

I'd have liked a week. Seven days, with little breaks for nourishment, that would have been what I needed to get myself used to it, to her. I mean somebody, a woman, who would . . .

His mind pitched back into the catalogue of daring things he'd wanted to try. With Amanda they were taken for granted, done. In fact, she had opinions on each one, along with small habits about their execution. Every time he tried to shock her, she shocked him back, stripped and splayed his favourite imaginings with her clinical enjoyment, her reality. All this, when he couldn't help wincing defensively the first time that she simply sucked him, even though she did so in a way he could not have anticipated that anyone ever would, with such a beautiful, soulless determination. She didn't hurt him, was only impeccably, firmly smooth, the close of her putting a tourniquet on the last of his sanity.

Very quickly, Amanda had worked him adrift from anyone

he could have thought he'd like to be. Greg remembered pulling back the curtain of her shower and seeing them both together, caught in the sweat of her bathroom mirror, his face staring back at him from a soaped configuration of shuddering pinks, his eyes unmistakably afraid.

He'd made it home by two and had ducked directly into the spare room, feeling beautifully bruised and scandalised. Still awake, he'd seen the dawn crawl across the ceiling and was almost surprised: a part of him had imagined the day would start differently now, or just not happen any more, everything necessary being over. A chill of anticipation jumped in his chest and perhaps this was the fear of discovery, of being forced to stop, or perhaps this was the fear of successful concealment and having to carry on. He didn't feel right, that was all—he didn't truly feel what he'd call right.

"Hung over?"

Naturally, at breakfast, he'd imagined that Karen would guess just what he'd done. She didn't.

"No, I think I'm getting flu." This was a gift and he meant it to be, the kind of lie that she enjoyed dissecting.

"You weren't in before one, I'm sure of that—this would be the flu to do with being up all night? Is this going to be a habit?"

I could get used to this, yes. It's nothing I should be scared of.

"No, it won't be a habit. The people from Sales—you know what they're like. I have to keep them happy, now and then."

It's only, currently, unfamiliar. I will get my second wind.

"Well, I'm glad you're keeping someone happy."

Greg, producing a suitably hangdog frown, had felt it curdle slowly when he glanced at Karen and found that she was smiling. She had decided to be teasing, but sympathetic. He couldn't begin to guess why and, frankly, didn't want to: he'd been too busy indulging a good, low beat of preparative thinking.

Spared

I can't plausibly get another evening soon enough. We could fuck on a Saturday, though, on a Saturday afternoon.

His wife had made him take a Beechams' powder and kissed him on the lips before he left for work. He had not felt remotely guilty, only slightly peculiar, as if he were moving in a predirected path, one that gripped him, gleeful, that left him raw and luminous, under the skin.

Greg had almost the same feeling now, a similar chafing of weighted expectancy. Although there was also the rash: that did have to be considered, a nervous thing he hadn't suffered from in years. In the fold of each elbow and on each shin he'd grown an irritable patch of crimson pinpricks. The doctor had given him ointment and, no doubt, the trouble would pass and Greg hadn't needed to hear it was stress-related. Sometimes, he'd stare at one patch or another and wonder if it might not cohere some morning, arranging itself to spell out Amanda's name. Or something worse, some message he didn't want to bear.

The digital red of his alarm clock showed 05:42 and he'd set it for six, but he might as well start, get up. Karen wouldn't surface before seven and by then he should really have everything done.

He didn't shave because it wasn't necessary, applied his ointment as directed on the tube, dressed quickly in a shirt and jeans and then took his bag from the bottom of the wardrobe. There wasn't much in it: a paperback, toothbrush and paste, another shirt, a pair of underpants and a Gideon's bible he'd stolen from a hotel recently. In the kitchen he added a packet of chocolate digestives and two apples, as if it really mattered what he took. When he'd been a promising youth of good moral fibre and hill-walking for his Duke of Edinburgh Awards, he'd always made sure to pack chocolate digestives and apples in his regulation haversack and he'd always come to no harm. Which was an adequate reason for taking them with him today—they might bring him safety, which was much more important than luck.

It was only half past six when he washed up his coffee cup and realised that he could go, because there was nothing else left for him to do. So he folded his raincoat over his arm, eased out of the back door and closed it, quiet behind him. A street away, he'd parked the car so that Karen wouldn't hear him when he started up the engine and drove off.

In an hour he was well clear of the city and rolling between dark stands of conifer. The daybreak had been smothered almost immediately in cloud and by ten it was raining hard, the peck of water overhead making his car seem cosy and sound. He turned on the radio and bounced across the frequencies, neither more nor less happy with any of them, but finally staying with one which conducted its business solely in Gaelic. This morning he wanted information that he could not understand, news that brought no disturbance, that didn't concern him. Every now and then a crow would fling itself into a sinking flight across the road, only to perch in a wet hump once it reached the sombre plush of the opposing trees.

When Greg noticed he was hungry he stopped in a small, rain-shuttered town and ate lunch in a gift shop café. The food was dreadful: oily tea, a mournful cheese sandwich, a forbidding raisin scone: but he didn't mind it, the nature of these things was the nature of these things and needn't be argued with, not any more. He loitered in amongst the available gifts along with a brace of sodden tourists and, inevitably, three hill-walkers. He bought the most pointless things he could find, then beamed while the assistant duly bagged a ceramic stag's head, a video tape of pipe bands and a pink Pringle golfing sweater.

"Is this for you?"

"Hm?"

"This is an extra large. A medium is quite big . . ." She eyed him appraisingly.

"That's fine. I'm not going to wear it." He grinned in what he hoped was an unbalanced way and eyed her in return. She didn't flinch.

Back in the car with his prizes, he pushed north, this time without turning on the radio.

The thing about this is, I can't be sure I'm right. In fact, I can be almost certain that I'm not.

*But if I **am** right.*

If I am right, I should be like this when it happens—with myself alone, contented. As close to contented as I get.

The idea must have nested in him for a while, only showing itself in needling little pieces, opening and spiralling out into his undefended sleep: here the taste of ash and there the sense of an absent sky. It finally, completely demanded his attention during his third time with Amanda—their hotel début. As far as Karen was concerned, he was leaving Glasgow fairly early one Saturday morning and driving to Edinburgh in order to meet a friend and get a cheap computer. The computer in question was already sitting in his office, bought with cash from a man in Sales. In reality, lovely reality, he was driving to Edinburgh fairly early one Saturday morning with Amanda and the intention of spending several hours in a hotel bed, or thereabouts. She would then take the train home, believing that he had a business dinner to attend, followed by a highly boring, all-Sunday conference. He would wait half an hour or so, check out with an excuse he'd never fully fixed on and go home once he'd picked up the computer. This was all rather complicated, but meant that he would have roughly five hours free for sex. Not counting whatever she did while he was driving.

As it turned out, she was an unexpectedly docile passenger.

"I don't like to distract you while you're driving."

"Distract away."

"I want all of your mind on what we're doing when we do it. I can wait."

So he had to, but as soon as they'd booked in and made it as far as the lift she compensated him for his patience.

"I'm not wearing any. Look."

"Jesus Christ, what if it . . . if someone comes in?" Although, as soon as he'd said it, he didn't care. "Fuck, that's gorgeous."

"I know."

His plan for the day only foundered, that waiting idea only slipped its claws inside, when he looked down at Amanda, bent over the chair, the pale flesh of her back cool under his palms. She felt so ideal against him and her spine made such an adorably undulating arch and there was absolutely no way she could turn her head to face him and meet his eyes, so that was when he told her, "Actually, I'm married."

Karen slowed their pace, but didn't stop, "I know," seemed to ask him to go deeper.

And he did so, bewildered, but rather more turned on than he had been all afternoon. "You *know?* How?" Rather more turned on than he could bear.

"You wear clothes you've picked to please someone else. They're not you, or not the whole of you."

He was going to come soon, if he wasn't careful. "And?" She was making it hard to be careful.

"We're fucking in a hotel room on a Saturday afternoon."

Which did it, which just did it, and left him faintly rocking, laid forward over her back, only gradually aware of a rolling sweat. "You don't mind?" His mouth seemed awfully gritty, odd.

"I'm here, aren't I?"

"But you won't . . ." It was tricky to speak.

"This is what I want."

"God." Words bouncing numbly in his skull, "I love you."

"You're very sweet."

Then Greg had rested across the bedspread with Amanda drowsily beside him and fitted to his shape remarkably. They had another two hours left and then she would set off home, but now he felt unnaturally sleepy and had begun to slip adrift when something seemed to hit him inside his head. An audible colour. A twist of light.

No. Not now. No.

That feeling of nearing extinction, the threat of heat under each of his lurching and unsatisfying dreams, the horrible conviction that he might reach out, unconscious, and touch the end of everything—here it was, with him, nakedly clear.

But that would be ridiculous.

Still, the moment slapped him awake, put a spasm in his neck.

"What's the matter?" The voice of Amanda. "Greg?" The woman who'd sprung the terminal lock, who'd shut him up alone with this.

"Nothing. I dreamed. Nothing."

"Do you want to start again, then? Hm?" The woman who could lick and tug and buck him away from it. "My greedy boy?" And now she'd have to, she owed him that.

So, although he didn't want to, not right then, although he actually needed to hug her, to hug someone, to be only held, "Oh . . . Yes," he made himself begin, "Why not?" because she would let him do that, "Yes." Because it was something to do. "Yes. Let's start again."

The end of days. Dear Lord, it's coming, the End of Days.

He'd pushed them both hard, harder than he liked, then decided to steal the bible as they were leaving.

"What on earth do you want that for?"

And he hadn't been able to tell her that this was foolish, but nevertheless, he would just feel safer if they had it with them in the car.

There are so many dates for the End of the World: you read about them in the paper when they've already gone and you hadn't been remotely aware, would have got no warning if they'd been right . . .

Nobody would know for sure. They couldn't. I couldn't.

Despite this, he'd dropped off Amanda, uplifted the computer and delivered it—and himself—home, with his head reeling round and round the list of every animal he thought he could remember that was said to sense coming earthquakes, or was forewarned of calamities.

And some people get this feeling when close relatives have died. And twins . . .

It was silly, though, to expect he'd be the only one, the only human to be aware of something this monumental. It was ridiculous. Ever since the day in the hotel he'd tried to think that.

And he did now, almost wholeheartedly, believe that his repeated premonitions and that single afternoon's burst of certainty did no more than prove he had a highly masochistic type of arrogance. This drive he was taking up north, it was primarily therapeutic. It really wasn't so very much to do with the end of the world. He was going away to relax—and his rash hadn't bothered him a bit since he'd started out—that was proof that he'd needed a break and here he was having it. From the coming midnight until the next, he'd decided that he would stay up here by himself, but it would be much more for a necessary rest than because he expected the close of recorded time.

I didn't believe the Millennium would trigger it, that would have been too neat. I wasn't anxious, then. Only averagely anxious, anyway. The way a person in my position would be anxious.

It was over eight months, now, that he'd known Amanda and

more than seven since they'd started to have sex. They'd settled into a pattern, her variation on normality.

"I don't need that. I've told you, I have what I want."

He'd tried to give her presents, "It's only a scarf . . . You don't have anything from me."

"Yes, I do." She started to unbuckle his belt.

"You wouldn't like to talk? Anticipation . . ." Sometimes, when she touched him, he thought it might happen again: the outbreak of emptiness, of ending. "We could go and have coffee and then . . ."

"We've done that."

"We've done this."

"But this is much more interesting. I don't suppose you've ever sodomised anyone."

"Ever . . . ? Uh, no." She would always do that, nudge through his fear and his better nature with something impossible to resist. "Do you think I will soon?" She made him forget himself.

"Yes, I do."

"Well, then . . ." He wanted to forget himself. "That's good."

The memory of it, of seeing her like that, made a touch of blood head south, plumbing his depths. Although it hadn't been something he'd enjoyed, so much as something he couldn't help wanting to do again. There was a great deal he couldn't help wanting to do again.

He turned the radio back on and retuned until he found some music, turned it up loud. A few miles further and Greg came to a section of road that was heavy with standing water. Careless for his engine, he drove at each pool directly and made plume after plume cape across his windscreen, each liquid impact scrabbling under his bodywork. He felt more peaceful afterwards and was calmed even more by the flat of the glen floor around him, the slow spin of mountains, parting and meeting before and behind.

Because there was a minute chance that it might be his last, he pulled off the road to watch what starts and licks of light the sunset could force through the cloud. He left the car and walked through the coarse, drizzly grass and into the whip and bounce of heather. He lay down as the valley dimmed to shadow and the rain fell on his face and he set himself aside from Amanda and Karen, from the misery of excitements, the bitter comforts, the whole thing. A curlew called and then there was a great peace. He fell into an utterly painless sleep.

What woke him was the cold. Greg was shivering before he was fully conscious. The ground around still smelt of summer, but the slight breeze was stern and he was soaked—all but the middle of his back. He got to his feet in a confusion of stiffness and chill and was immediately terrified by the total dark, couldn't see his watch, couldn't tell if he'd moved past midnight, if this was it. Then he tripped on a high sprawl of roots and fell where he could see his headlamps, still mercifully there and bright in a way which implied he hadn't fucked the battery by leaving them to burn.

I didn't want this to be over, not everything. I hate it, but I didn't want it to have gone away. Or maybe I didn't want it to leave me behind.

Safely in the car, he started up the engine without a hitch, changed his shirt and was forced to put on the pink sweater, just to get warm. Its sleeves were long enough to act as mittens, which was a mercy.

I didn't want it to leave me behind.

Gently, he circled and jolted down into the road, got under way again, his watch showing just past two in the morning, which meant he hadn't paid attention as well as he might. This could be the big day, could be coiled right down around the start of the big moment. Any second now. Already, The End could have taken him unawares. He could have missed it and never known.

But I'm wrong. Nothing's going to happen. Nothing's going to leave me and I really ought to be certain of that. I've got no proper cause for doubt.

I'm wrong and by midnight tomorrow, I'll know that I'm wrong.
That should make me happy.
By midnight tomorrow, that's how I should be.
Happy.
That's how I should be.

Awaiting an Adverse Reaction

It's unmistakable, organic, the flavour of something live.

"Oh, that's dreadful."

She shifts in her chair while the doctor pads across and to his fridge.

"Dreadful?"

"The taste. I don't get a sweetie for after?"

"No." He turns back with a blur of smile. "No sugar lump to go with it and no sweetie for afterwards." Quietly teasing between the slim and softly shining shelves, "Sugar is bad for you and here we don't ever dispense what is bad for you."

"A small piece of fruit, then?"

"This is a surgery, not a restaurant." He coughs out a small laugh and decides to risk, "And that's a Scottish medicine—if it tastes bad, it must be working," before glancing to check if she takes him in good part.

She grimaces back, not entirely unhappily, and swims the flavour round her tongue, hoping it will weaken. Under the tickle of spreading salt, the cold initial weight of the vaccine, there is something familiar about the taste. She knows that if she concentrates, identification will come.

Her doctor advances, hands benevolently folded round a

stack of suitably chilled inoculations: the start of any truly happy holiday.

"I'll need the use of both your arms." Laying out his packages and snapping the first needle free: "Tetanus and hepatitis this side . . ." he grins curatively; "diphtheria and typhoid that."

Something about his casual enumeration of plagues is strangely enjoyable, a comfort to her. She is being made safe; a part of her bloodstream is welcoming something foreign, so that none of her will go wrong when she takes all her body abroad.

She swallows and briefly considers the matter of Gordon. Gordon will not be made safe, because he will not go with her, because he does not like abroad. He does like her, but not abroad. She does like abroad. The thought of abroad is something she likes very much.

"I won't hurt." The doctor draws a careful epidemic up inside his syringe.

"I know you won't. I will."

She rolls up her sleeves, hoping that she can offer him flesh high enough on her arms. She would rather not take off her blouse. In the past, her doctor's acts of examination have been both medical and polite; a nurse discreetly attending, should any especially intimate explorations be required. Even so, undressing always seems more awkward than being undressed—having to stumble her clothes off while the doctor slips outside and the nurse presses breaths through the disinfected silence and shifts tinily on white crêpe soles, observing. Nothing to enjoy. But that won't happen today.

He nods, "Good," then pushes a pinching kind of pain inside her skin; holds it, dabs around it, withdraws and dabs again. "Terribly bad?"

"No. Not bad at all."

"Mm. I am actually quite good at giving injections. I still

practise, you see. Others I could mention do not. How's the polio doing?"

"I can still taste it. In fact, I think it's getting worse. It reminds me of . . . I don't know what." He slips in another needle, while she thinks. *That wasn't fair.*

"Some people would rather not know what's going on."

"It's my arm, I like to keep tabs on it."

"I quite understand. Other side and then we're done. We just ask you to wait for a few minutes more, in case there's an adverse reaction."

As soon as he says this, she feels a rush in her circulation, a burst of strangeness, but nothing she would call adverse. Her flesh is being fortified like wine, science defending her against nature more deeply with every prick.

"You're getting tense—this will be painful if you don't relax."

"Sorry."

"Not to worry. You've been a very patient patient. And. Last one. There. Will you be going away for long?"

"A month." A month away from Gordon, during which time she will try to phone him and will certainly write him postcards and may nevertheless experience increasingly serious bouts of what she might well call relief. She can feel her symptoms building, even now.

"Terrific. A month."

One whole month of perhaps incurable relief.

They probably will fire her when she gets back home. Already, she has calculated the likelihood of summary dismissal. She finds that it doesn't scare her—not in the way that disease might, or a month staying here with Gordon and his list of things they shouldn't talk about.

"Yes, I've saved up my holiday time"; pausing, recalling the polio taste and where she met it once before, knowing it, making a smile, "And I'm taking four days off sick."

"Really?" He pauses to look quintessentially medical: phial held high, a glimmer at his needle and naturally chill, but very steady hands. "What will be wrong, in your professional opinion?" His voice relaxes into a type of wink—his eyes being unable to do the same, for reasons of professional distance and confidence.

"Wrong? Oh, probably flu. Probably not typhoid, or hepatitis, or—"

"Or tetanus, or diphtheria, or polio. Yes, I think that flu would probably be best. In my professional opinion."

Or polio. She licked against her teeth and smiled again. On their second anniversary, last spring, when Gordon had asked her to do it and she'd finally agreed, when he'd got his way—this is how he'd tasted. The gagging nudge in her throat, repeating, and then warmed polio vaccine. It's just like him.

"As you're away so long . . ." The doctor ponders, above her notes, "I could write out your next prescription for TriNovum."

"For?"

"Your contraceptive."

Her passport for Gordon to travel, pregnancy free.

"Oh yes, thank you."

"No problems, periods normal?"

"No problems at all." She can say this because it will be true soon and might as well be now: her hopes proving unexpectedly resistant to all antidotes.

She waits as he checks the pressure of her altering blood, not minding the hard fit of the cuff, and taking—for the sake of politeness—the prescription for an oral contraceptive she may never use, at least not with Gordon.

"Thank you."

"We aim to please." He opens the door so that she can start to go away. "Do have a nice holiday."

"I will."

She is aware that, when she speaks, her breath is vaguely coloured with the taste of something not unlike seminal fluid. She is aware of something not unlike the cloy and tang of spunk. She is aware that her husband has the flavour of a tentatively sweetened disease. But, finally, it seems she has developed a complete immunity.

An Immaculate Man

"Yes." Hot little word, slightly angry, very solid, very meant. "Yes."

All she said.

How old was she? He couldn't tell by looking. The paperwork gave her birth date and it wasn't exactly beyond him to work out that she was ten, but he would have guessed twelve, or older, because she seemed so tired and so deeply still. This meant he must, somewhere, associate exhaustion and immobility with age. Certainly, they were associated with *his* age.

*Ten. Jesus God, what in hell has happened to her yet? What can she possibly **know**? And here she is landed with **this**.*

Clothes like her mother's: good and clean, but distressed, unhappily mismatched. The pair of them were dressing on the run; out of suitcases and despair, he would imagine. The mother wore the wrong shoes for this weather and she knew it and didn't care. Sometimes separation would take people that way, making them want to act biblically, to seem on the brink of rending garments and putting ashes in their hair. He'd seen it before.

The daughter was staring again, focusing herself at one meaningless point on the top of his desk and giving him her forehead instead of her face. She was trying some type of self-hypnosis to keep his best efforts away from her mind when he'd already made it quite clear that he was on her side completely and only had to ask unpleasant questions to determine what she genuinely wished. The comprehensive and accurate fulfilment of all her desires was almost undoubtedly well within his gift. She could and would get what she wanted to get. This was something which rarely, if ever, happened throughout the course of anybody's life and he was offering it to her now, as her perfect right. He was her *friend.*

"I'm your friend, you do know that, don't you?"

She leaned further forward, her elbows resting on her knees and he somehow doubted she could hear him, although a brief shudder showed in her back when he spoke. Was she permanently round-shouldered, or simply wincing herself temporarily away from things? She wouldn't be so pale in the summer, he was sure, and she would know how to smile. Of course she would.

The mother shifted her weight, looking, as was customary, close to tears. She never did cry, though. Considerate. Still, no need to test her endurance beyond its strength. He'd already got the answers he required.

"Fine. Well, thank you. You've been really very clear. If you want to stay with your mother and not g—" The child's attention leaped at him, made him swallow half his word "—go to your father. Sorry. *Not* go to your father." He felt the air unclench. "Then we'll try to ensure that happens. Fine. I'll fix it. That's what I do: I get things fixed." He raised his head to the mother, cooled his voice, gave it the proper, professional pace. "If you don't mind . . . Excuse me for one moment."

The girl didn't stir as he passed her, although his jacket must have tapped her arm, at least. Prudence suggested he should pause by the mother, bend vaguely at his waist and accept her brief, ferocious smile which fought to suggest that her daughter loved her and that she was, therefore, still essentially lovable.

He nodded and pursed his lips to imply his agreement and support, or at least an understanding reached, or simply to let her know that he was deserting her now with good reason. His absence would allow them to talk and let their feelings calm. They could then be appropriately loving with each other and settle down before he came back to join them in the ghastly little interview room with its overheating and underlighting and dying rubber plant. Jesus, it was appalling—the pastel motel carpet and the stolidly tasteful furniture intended to imply reliability and a courteous use of clients' fees, unblemished by unreasonable charging and other extravagance. He really did have to go—the human mind could only bear so much terracotta ragging.

His offer of tea was refused. "Something for the girl, then. Milk? Lemonade? Actually, we have none."

"No, really, Mr. Howie. We're all right."

Rather than pat the mother's shoulder, which he felt she wouldn't like, Howie straightened and nodded again, confidingly.

"Perhaps if I might telephone tomorrow, we could discuss the aliment. And I do feel Mr. Simpson's comments over custody won't come to much: pursuing it could only represent a pointless expense." Her eyes wailed at him suddenly. "Back in one moment, Mrs. Simpson. Excuse me. Fine."

Out in the passageway, Howie felt cleaner immediately. He detested the fug and the panic, the terrible malleability of words—all of the paraphernalia that straggled around clients and the law. His working life had started to have a particular, dragging smell, like the after-prison-visit tang he'd never been able to clean from his suits in his bad, old criminal days.

He paused, pushed back his shoulders till his backbone let out a series of grinding snaps. How best to pass the time . . . He could either make a phone call, or take a leak. The leak won.

He washed his hands and face before he started, trying to get the misery out from under his fingernails and cool his skin.

Then Salter came in. Howie knew it was him without looking. Salter had a way of half whistling and half exhaling between his teeth while he walked about. Some people found this annoying, of course, but Howie took it as a kind of reassurance. The sound was almost melodious, mildly contented and instantly recognisable. Salter's sound was a part of what made him; like the quiet shoes, usually suede, and the little gap in his lower teeth that he worried between with his tongue while he was thinking. If you imagined him at any time while he wasn't there, these were things that might very easily spring to mind. But above all, the whistling.

Howie stood, breathing inaudibly, moved his thumb a touch along his prick and then moved it back again, feeling foolish and observed. Salter. A good man, Salter. He looked as if he might be confided in with safety. If one ever had anything suitable to confide. The base of Howie's neck felt strange, it tickled a bit.

Before a pressure dunted hard in at his chest and he looked down, half expecting to find blood, or something awful and ridiculous like that. A tightness rippled implacably round his ribs.

Fuck. Oh, shit. Oh, fuck.

A man's arms were fixing him, hands buckled together above his breast bone. And he could see where his own hands were locked clumsily in place, one of them holding his prick while he still pissed, because he couldn't help it, because once you've started pissing and passed the point, you really can't stop and you just have to keep on pissing until you're emptied out. This was unfair.

It's a joke. It must be. Please.

He shook his head without meaning to and felt a high, inappropriate noise burst in his throat.

This is a fight. But this is Salter. This is Salter's hands. I can't fight Salter. He'll win.

A definite exhalation nudged past him and then Salter's chin dropped, solid on Howie's shoulder. Howie shut his eyes and felt his thinking rock and swim. Salter's body steamed in close, one of its legs bending warmly to fit the soft curl behind Howie's knee. Another squeezed in to the side, thigh to thigh. Howie's breath fought back against the swell of another man's lungs while his scalp greased over with an unwanted sweat.

When you're drowning, it must be like this.

He couldn't shift his hand. Even though he'd stopped now, was done, he couldn't move. He couldn't put himself away.

"Howie."

The voice loped in like a blow while Howie felt the shape of his own name working soft, fierce changes in another man's mouth, set at his cheek. He felt himself waver in a grasp of precarious flight.

Please. You mustn't do this. You don't mean what I want you to mean.

But he leaned back in any case and let himself rest on a body he couldn't trust. He twitched his neck to turn, to speak, but Salter bore up against him like a good, new faith, like the fulfilment of a promise putting itself within his reach.

"Sssh."

The rush of that tobogganed down Howie's ear to fracture him completely, bits and pieces of thinking span off, crumpled, were entirely misplaced, with all the time Salter's arms there and deciding to tense harder, to constrict.

Howie coughed up a burst of nonsense, shrill as his brain. "I can't . . . I can't . . . when you're holding . . ." Nerves lit up in his spine, "Is this . . . Did I do? . . ." caught the thin, round pressure from one of Salter's hips, "Please," the rising line of his prick. "Please."

"Sssh."

And then nothing more. Howie stumbled back, slipped into a queasy turn, suddenly and coldly freed. Salter was already reaching for the door and leaving and not speaking and not making an effort to signal, to communicate in even the smallest sense: no turn of the head, no self-consciousness in the shoulders, no especial grace or tenderness in the curl and turn of his hand; no goodbye, no clue.

Howie still cradled himself, now facing the doorway and knowing a thick lift of want was taking his weight from his fingers. He was yowling with solidity, pressing his thought up and forward into one or two beads of clarified despair. Before lack and embarrassment and, almost undoubtedly, fear slammed at him and started to wither his hopes.

If I'd done something back.

To either side, reflections snagged his attention with mirrored angles on a man who blinked, who had bewildered hair, who was shrivelling, retreating in his hand and licking his lips and licking his lips.

If I'd done something back.

The interview room was silent and probably calmer although he was in no state to tell. He noticed, as he walked in, what must be a line of piss, staining a stripe across his shoe.

"Is there anything?" His voice sounded no different, his clothing was not in disarray, but how long had he been away for? Anxiety crept across his palms. "Was I . . . ? I didn't keep you waiting, did I?"

Two pairs of identically grey-blue eyes blinked at him neutrally. The mother shook her head.

"Well, there were no . . . messages. So. Since you've had a while to think. Are there any other points you'd like to make?" He tried to meet the daughter's eyes and didn't manage. Really, he should get behind the desk and hide his shoe. But he'd have to show them out soon—better stay where he was. Once the leather dried it would be fine, most likely. "Questions? No? Good."

He tried an unwieldy smile and allowed his arms to initiate vaguely ushering movements. Mother and daughter took his hint rather more keenly than was complimentary. Anxious to leave the room. Anxious to leave him. Not surprising, really— he must look remarkably like a man whose hands were now slithering with confusion, whose shirt was sopped and plastered between his arms and the shoulders of his jacket, and down against the small of his back, and who wanted to fuck, just to fuck, just to fuck.

No, to come. No, to fuck—the one you can't do on your own.

"Take care, then. Both. And I'll call tomorrow. Would tomorrow be good? We have the new number. You'll be . . ." He didn't have to offer them affection, they didn't want affection, they wanted appropriately professional behaviour and sound advice. But if they didn't go now he would scream. Then he would run and beat his head through the window and scream very much louder for a long time. "Bye, then. Bye."

Howie turned from them in the corridor and began the walk to his office, stupidly afraid of what it might hold. Afraid, to be more precise, of finding his office utterly undisturbed: without a note, a change of his usual good order, somebody in there and waiting for him.

The girl and her mother—should have called them a cab. It'll still be sleeting. You should have thought. You should have taken care.

Almost at his office door, he caught again the feel of a brush at his cheek and recalled that Salter didn't always shave quite thoroughly. There would often be those few hairs overhung by the broadest part of lower lip. The effect was not untidy but it drew the eye.

You'll have to go out yourself soon, get home for the evening. A cab might be the best idea, this weather. No need to decide now, though. It could pass, these things sometimes do.

His office was just as he'd left it, not touched.

I almost wore a pullover, this morning. I wish I had. It would have been soft for him. It would have kept his smell. Jesus.

*He could have been joking. He **must** have been joking. Except I know he was serious.*

I hate my room, it is too small for me—too small, even for me.

I don't look gay. I don't act gay. I don't ever say that I am gay.

There are gay people with the firm, people who are openly orientated in that direction. Barnaby is gay and, I think, Curtis. They are not mocked or humiliated, they are only themselves and accepted and relatively efficient—no more or less appreciated than any of the rest of us. I could be gay here in safety, like them, I do know that. I don't hate the idea, the actions, the thought. Being gay as a concept, that's probably something I love. I do, very probably, love that I am gay. I only hate me.

But Salter, I was sure he wasn't, hadn't—I thought he had another type of life. I thought I remembered hearing—something I now can't recall. I don't listen enough. Keep oneself to oneself, then there's no need to lie, confess, confide, that stuff people do when they don't mind finding, being found out. I don't want to be out.

*I **didn't** want to be out. I didn't want to be found. I didn't want to find no one was looking.*

I should not, do not, should not wish to find out about Salter. I do not wish to be told this is impossible.

But this couldn't be more impossible than it is now.
And this couldn't be more wonderful. Really.

At the far end of the building, a Hoover muttered and worried to life. Howie should go. All he'd done since he left Mrs. Simpson was fumble blankly through his files and almost trash a phone call. He'd pleaded flu to excuse himself and then settled back to staring at his hands. His fingers were tapered, not stumpy, which he seemed to remember was a sign of sensitivity.

Ha, ha, ha, ha.

He should get his coat. There was no point waiting.

He really should go home.

Where it was just exactly warm and light enough and he'd done the paper and paintwork himself so each room was absolutely the way he wanted and ideal for being comfortable in when alone. Alone being the standard state: what the firm's computers would recognise as his default.

Bath. Relax. And then the good dressing gown, the long one and no slippers because they were a sign of decay and shuffling and the wholly pathetic type of domesticity.

Howie came to rest in his living room, hot and washed, but still coated with recollections that watched and pried. His movements were hobbled and muffled with self-consciousness, as if the attention his mind was giving another body was being consistently equalled by that other body's mind, as if his substance was being pondered, fingered, in thoughts beyond his reach. He found himself folding his arms, shifting, shielding his face from the glare of nothing and no one.

When he went to bed early, it was only for some kind of privacy, only for that.

*What does he **mean**?*

Howie's ankles had started to tingle.

*From a look—you can't tell from a look. But a look like **that**, it couldn't be an accident.*

His whole feet were hot now, wet, even the soles, which was ludicrous—as if he'd stepped into a basin when all he'd done was answer a smile with a smile. A pleasant insanity was flaring and hopping up from rib to rib, lifting him, lifting him entire.

Dear God. I'll touch him. How can I not.

They were tucked in together in the tea room, slipping and straining to dodge the hot metal of the urn, the unstable clutter in the sink, the thrum of space closing and yawning between unavoidable, small contacts. Salter had good hands, no one could deny it: those tapering fingers allegedly so indicative of a sensitive man, the beginnings of dark hair turning close round the curve of the wrist, nipping in under the shirt cuff.

A man's hands. The things to hold, the size to hold, to move under. These hands, like my hands, like part of a better me.

"Not much room in here, eh, Howie?"

Cheeky smile, naughty smile, bad, bad, bad boy's smile. God, let me not be imagining this.

"No. No, it's . . ." Facing each other and overly near. Howie thought they were overly near. "I suppose it's . . ." Although, of course, not near enough. The need to reach forward was slapping and twisting in Howie like a flag. "Difficult."

"Mm. Difficult."

Salter lifted his mug and drank, slowly, perhaps tenderly, perhaps only being cautious of the heat. He swallowed and a liquid motion eased down the length of his throat. The thumb of his free hand rose to dab at his lips, to press, to pause.

Please.

Howie began to understand the turning of the world, the slewing of continents and oceans, the problem of ever, at any time, keeping one's feet.

Please.

Then he let himself have his way and pushed his hand out through the thick, unpredictable air until he could reach the side of Salter's face. Leaning forward, he tried to hold steady against the broad mayhem of information roaring in from that one moving touch: the warm of flesh, above and below the shaving line: the upward twitch of a blink: a small resistance of bristle and then an ear's gape, its soft lobe and cool rim: the fabulous close nap of his hair set trim at the start of his skull and the final, searing, glorious skin, whole and smooth and taut on Salter's neck.

Oh, Jesus.

Salter shut his eyes, rocked his head back and to the side, pressed Howie's palm.

He'll stop me. He'll move away. He'll stop me. I won't. He will.

"Stop." Salter's voice was low in his throat, gentle and, somehow, amused. "Oh, do stop." An approving murmur, while Salter slipped a glance over Howie, something about it suggestive of ownership. The overhead strip light glared down between them, showed the bright grains of steam leaping up from their mugs, swirling like flame. "But I mean it now. Please. Stop."

Howie brought his hand away. Hope bobbed absurdly in his throat when Salter stepped nearer, then picked up the milk. "Need a little drop more of this stuff, I think. You?"

"Mm?" Common sense dodging round his kidneys, out of sight, out of mind "I?"

"Do you need any more?" And a kiss so fast and light against Howie's cheek that it might not have happened, but it did, it indisputably did. Salter gave him the milk and walked away.

Howie blundered back to his office, slopping his mug and smiling—he hoped—in only a minor way.

I'm too hard. I can't be like this and not do something about it. If I sit, if I sit down and look out of the window and think of work, it'll maybe go.

Like fuck.

I HAVE AN ERECTION I DIDN'T MAKE. I am not responsible. This belongs to Brian Salter. I want to give this to Brian Salter. I want him to have this. Me.

One of the secretaries passed him with a nod, looking studiously overworked.

"Afternoon, Mrs. Carstairs, blessings upon both you and the State Mental Hospital bearing your name. I have, in case you wondered, a massive fucking hard-on, caused by my immediate superior, dark horse and senior partner of this parish, Mr. Brian Salter. YES."

Howie became a collector. In a handful of attentive days he snatched up nods in the hallway, a hand brushed in the midst of other company while the morning shrugged under him, dizzy. He also kept an inventory of pauses where explanations might have been shown, or even one more kiss, perhaps a little longer, fuller, more likely to offer a taste. It took very little to dash him, but he couldn't complain—it took so very, very little to make him shine.

Christmas bore down on the city and even on the firm, which allowed its interview rooms and its offices and the secretaries' open-plan pen to sport a familiar ration of weary foil and tinsel. No mistletoe.

By half past four the city sky would smudge out to a coffee-coloured blank and the knowledge of night closing round them all would fill Howie up with risky possibilities. He'd taken to working late, even after the cleaners had gone, busying himself in his office, alone, available, ulterior motivation quietly harrying. Everyone knew he was here, that this was now his habit. He made sure that everyone knew.

And each evening, he would sit with his door a quarter-inch ajar and listen to the building as it came to rest. The silence never broke, although his heart would jolt in him, now and then, at some distant disturbance. He would beat missives towards conclusion and tease couples' lives apart, then make himself a fresh coffee, drink it as his mind lowered into heat.

I know how to do it. I never have, but I've heard the talk. In the cubicle, it would be easy, I'm sure. A bit of conversation, then we'd walk past the stalls and lock ourselves in together. Hope no one else turns up outside. But if they do, we wait until they've gone. It's not a problem, that's the whole point about doing it this way. We would be safe—effectively safe—at any time. I'll have to get a bag.

The bag is important. I need a good one, the type they put nice clothes in, one of the kind made of something like almost thin card, instead of plastic. Paper would be no good. We'd need something rigid. Definitely. Stiff.

*We close the door and I fold out the bag and step in it. No. I'd be taking him, so that wouldn't work. I ask **him** to step in the bag and then I put the lid down on the bog and sit. Sit in front of him, head at the height of his waist. Anyone looks there's one pair of feet where they should be, a little spot of shopping in evidence and the right number of feet. But I'm inside, feet either side of the bag and lifting my eyes to his face and he wouldn't have to do anything, not if he didn't want to, I'd do it all. Take down his fly. Calm, definite moves—too light is annoying and too rough is too rough. As if it was me. Touch him as if he was me, strip down to the final layer and lift him out, probably **let** him out, really, the pressure of blood already there and doing its bit to make him spring. To watch him spring, just to watch him.*

But then I'd want his prick on my forehead, the silk roll of that, heavy and tight and a fat weight in it. Not for too long, though—kissing his balls, it would be while I did that, I'd press him and rest him so the tip of him touched my hair. Maybe more than the tip, I'm not receding. I've got more hair than when I was twenty. The same amount, anyway.

He could stroke my hair. Put his hands down on my head. Move me. Steer me. If he wanted.

I don't know how he'd smell. A bit pissy maybe—cloth, or talc,

*or soap, or nothing but him, straining. Private skin and sweat—
private and only for us.*

*I do still remember that. Breathing round the rush of a prick,
licking down everything it wants and rolling, nodding for it, bowing
to it. I don't see how a woman could do that. I don't see they could
know how.*

"And?"

"Mrs."

Howie's mind scrambled over itself to get off and away,
stumbling, kicking over his clutter of hopes.

"Mr. and Mrs." Mrs. Carstairs repeated herself, frowning
gently, as if he'd become inconveniently stupid. Which of course
he had. Recently, he'd become more stupid than he could believe.

He nodded and found it strangely hard to stop. "Mr. and
Mrs. Salter. Fine. Any little Salters?"

*You don't want that answer. You don't want to know. Leave it,
for fuck's sake.*

"Any?"

"You know. Family. What a thought, eh. With those
genes . . ." he mugged badly, something cold and liquid rising in
his skull. "Just a joke."

Ha, ha, ha, ha.

"I can't think why I've never sent out cards before. Then I
would have known all this. I just don't really . . . like Christmas."

"Well, I'm never sure if I do, I suppose. The idea's always
better than the reality, isn't it."

"Always. Yes."

"Actually, I think he has a little boy—Mr. Salter."

*Hold firm on her face, keep looking in her eyes, smile. This is not
important, this is not any of your business. But you had to fucking
ask, didn't you? Fucker.*

"Oh? Nice." *Still smiling, get a grip.* "And is that everyone?"

"There's the usual big card for the cleaners. Unless you want to do something for them yourself."

"No."

"Then, no, I didn't think so."

"Don't want to overdo it. You can have too much Christmas spirit." *Smile.*

"Yes." She was giving him a kind look and he could only assume this was because he seemed such a sad, old bastard—all of a sudden wanting to join in, pass out office Christmas cards, have his share in the festivities.

"Yeah. No need to overdo it. No indeed. Thanks for the help, Mrs. Carstairs."

"No trouble."

Which she said with a dab of affection that he couldn't acknowledge, being already in motion and heading for the Gents. Guaranteed privacy.

Ha, ha, ha, ha.

Bolt the door and lose it. Sob. The effort vacuum-pumping at your own lungs—no noise happening, just a heaving rock—until the next stage bangs in, and your voice is back, ridiculous and tiny with pain. You want no one to come in and hear you, but you don't want to be alone.

Ha, ha, ha, ha.

He tried to believe this would break from him and be over, get all the nonsense out of the way. There was the toilet roll to clean his face with when he'd stopped. It wouldn't be so bad, only a necessary release.

Except he didn't stop. Howie yanked breath in between his teeth, wincing at the hiss, and cried and folded his arms around his head and cried and punched his fist against the door and cried. He sat on the toilet with the lid down, the way he would for Salter, if Salter had been there, and he cried.

He might come in. Not now. In a bit. I'll get myself back together.

*Then he might be there when I come out and I might not have to say
anything, because things would be clear in my face. He could take me in
his arms and I could take him in mine. Take him. What I need. Fuck.*
   Shut the fuck up.
   The way no one's ever done it.
   Shut the fuck up.

A conference saved him, temporarily. He stood in for a last-
minute drop-out, volunteered as he never had before, and let
himself be cornered in a bland mediation centre for three puerile
days.

   Once there, Howie was not a co-operative group member.
He made no effort to share his experiences with his allocated
partner, took no notes in the lectures, but dawdled his pen across
the paper in an openly surly scrawl. In the breaks for meals or
biscuits, he would keep to himself, appear to be reading: he no
longer had an appetite. His sleep had left him, his attention span
diminishing, the most mundane tasks defeated by bouts of
excessive weariness. And there was nothing he could do to prevent this: his body's outrage at himself, his foolishness. He could
even—shamefully, softly—feel himself enjoy his weight loss, his
merciful inability to think, the others' attempts at concern when
they thought he was ill. There was nothing wrong with him, of
course: he was simply discovering things he could still do, the
changes he did have the power to make, his signs of love.

   The first day he was due back in at work, he woke up at five
in the morning with an absence lying heavy on him from the
back of his throat to his balls. He thought about pride, about
dignity—the way they were overrated.

   I hope that you are feeling better now.
   All the best, Brian.

The note was lying in wait for him on his desk. He'd managed the corridor and the secretaries and the enquiries after his time away and then two sentences' worth of ink dropped him cold where he stood. He wanted to go home and to resign and to go into Brian Salter's office and thank him so much for caring, or beat in his fucking, prick-teasing head. But the phone rang and he let it take him into what he knew: the law and how it worked in people. He was safe, he was making do.

Hours congealed around him: made one day, two, a week: and he learned that he need not meet Salter's eyes and that even a wafer of air could insulate him from the bite, the lunge of Salter's skin. He didn't always want to retch when he moved away without making a contact, without asking for acknowledgement. But when Salter came into his room, soft shoes hushing at the carpet, hands slow and graceful when they closed the door and made them the only two there, then he didn't in any way know what to do.

"But I do know—you should come."

Resolution was shuddering loose from each of Howie's joints. Salter seemed nervous, *Brian* seemed nervous, a raw edge in his face. "Come."

"I don't think. I can't. I've never gone."

"I know." Salter flicked a glance at Howie, testing. "You've been missed. This year . . ." He drove his hands into his pockets. "It's Christmas. People go to parties."

"I don't."

"But you could. If I asked. Otherwise I'll be there on my own."

"I shouldn't."

"But you will."

"If I . . . What would I . . . You're not being . . . fair."

"Thanks." Salter sent him a grin, watched it work in him,

started to turn for the door and then stepped back. Howie understood he would do nothing but sit still now and let expectation lash him open while Salter walked up to his desk and then round it to find him.

He closed his eyes, parted his lips for the kiss, not sure that it would come, but it did. And then here he was, Howie, Peter Howie, easing in the muscle of Brian's tongue, sucking until it spoke in him, flirting and giving. It felt like the way Brian was: clever, certain, funny, irreplaceable. He was drawn forward himself then, into a perfect comfort. They sounded so loud, so unmistakably like kissing, so much like a proper couple, tailspinning off towards a fuck.

He was aware of being happy.

"One day," Salter spoke into Howie's hair, "I'll make you so full." Then he gentled himself away and the start of that idea arched and exploded in Howie like a Very light. He gleamed with it all week, shivered whenever he let it out to play.

Stupid fuck. What are you doing? Have you thought what you're fucking doing? Are you insane?

No, I am just desperate. That's enough.

By the time he got there, the pub was more than full: God knew how many office parties hazing and blundering into each other. Howie stood quite near to the entrance for a while, checking faces and wondering if he should stay.

I should go home and change. I'm all wrong.

Tarting up for him, silly fucker. Trying too hard. No one will see you anyway, it's so bloody dark.

Music broiled around him like a physical force and a volley of cheering lurched up, faded. He tried to enjoy the pound of amplified percussion in his chest and knew he should leave. There was nothing he could have here, nothing he would be allowed.

But he stepped down and started to wade forward through the barrage of bodies, because going home after coming so far would make him seem more feeble than he cared to be.

That's him. Shit. That's. That was the side of his face, it was, but I can't tell which way he's gone. The thought of Salter bellowed through Howie, seized the muscle in his legs.

Fuck. This is ridiculous. Pathetic. He was shaking down into a sweat, hands thumping with senseless blood. *I'll fall. And I don't want to. People will think I've been drinking.*

A bed, mine. If I could take him to my bed. Once. He could do anything. There's nothing I couldn't take or wouldn't want.

A hand caught his elbow. "You made it. I am glad." Salter. In a lovely sweater, jeans. Howie sensed himself either too heavy, or too light. He wanted to answer but couldn't.

Salter tilted his head to one side and let half a smile slip for the two of them to share. "I wasn't sure if you would."

"Nor was I."

"But you're not thinking of leaving . . ."

"No." *Liar.*

"Listen, I'm in the middle of something inappropriately businesslike with Billy Parsons—"

"That's OK."

"But I'll be back."

"That's fine. I'll be here." Yelling into the din, this was absurd.

"Good. Make sure you are." Then, as he passed Howie's shoulder, Salter breathed out a shot to the brain, to the cock, "I'll smooth out that frown for you later. Don't go."

Howie watched Salter retreating and then being taken into a ring of conversations, his hands making lazy curves whenever he spoke.

He's maybe not wonderful, only good; but my kind of good. Sweet. I'd take care of him, I would.

Let me take your wife and child and make them go. Let me ruin your life, because I don't have one. Let me love you as much as I'd like.

Fuck, if he's asking for it, then he must want it, mustn't he?

I want it.

He made me.

Please. I think I can do it. Please, let me try.

For ten or fifteen minutes, people Howie worked with came up and threw words at him. He listened with such small attention, he felt sure they would be offended and move away, but they smiled and milled around him, as if they were entirely satisfied. He had to go.

"No, you don't." Mrs. Carstairs, patting his shoulder. "You can't leave now. I've come to fetch you."

"What?"

"To fetch you. I'm being a good secretary. Even if I am off duty." She offered him a hoarse, off-duty laugh. Perhaps a bit of a goer, Mrs. Carstairs.

"Fetch me?"

"No questions. Come on."

So he let her tug him between knots of talk, glistening faces, daytime acquaintances relishing their annual chance to slur into lechery. Naturally, Salter had sent her and was waiting, neatly ready to give her the Christmas peck on the cheek, his eyes finding Howie while he kissed.

"Just a thank-you would have been fine." Was she blushing? Howie thought she might be.

"Don't worry. We'll be back to normal after the break." Salter the genial boss, tolerant of humour, but ultimately serious.

She'll go and we'll be alone.

Mrs. Carstairs giggled. "Don't remind me. Well . . ." Howie knew she'd rather not kiss him and shook her hand before she had to try.

And I'll leave soon, because I have to. We'll leave.

"Merry Christmas, Mrs. Carstairs. Mary."

Please.

"Merry Christmas, Mr. Howie. You'll be fine now."

His body stammered while he tried to understand her. "I'll be . . . ?"

"You wanted to go early. Brian—Mr. Salter—is leaving early, too. You can share a cab. That's why I . . ." She let her explanation drift away. "You know. You'll work it out." Howie realised she was quite drunk. "Night, night. Merry Christmas."

Salter scooped him in with an arm round his shoulder.

I can't.

"The wonderful thing about Christmas . . ." Their hips met. Beautifully. "It lets men be mates."

"Please." *Please.*

"Sssh. We'll go out and hail a taxi. Get you home."

"I—"

Please.

"That's what you wanted, isn't it? To go home."

Tell him now, tell him. You have to be sensible, have to stop.

"Isn't that what you want?"

No. No. No.

"Isn't it?"

"Yes."

Hot little word.

Not Anything to Do with Love

I wouldn't want to say so, but it's freezing in here. I suppose most people usually don't notice, not wanting to take their coats off, and being preoccupied, God knows: or this could even be an intentional chill, I mean, the last thing you'd want to consider right now is heat. Still, it doesn't seem a sign of kindness—a cold crematorium—more like forcing the bereaved to do their mourning inside a bad joke.

And, if I think of that, the possibility of giggling does tickle very briefly, but I frown against it, I resist. I do almost always laugh when I shouldn't, in fact *because* I shouldn't. Not that I'm cruel, I don't feel cruel, I've only decided that, since bad things happen without my permission, I will refuse to let them also make me sad.

I can't help it, either, the laughing: solemn gatherings, slow ballads, pompous orations, any person or occasion that assumes I'll offer my unreserved respect: I tend to find them all hysterical in the end. Especially if someone similar is there to set me off. They don't have to do much: I recognise what it looks like when somebody's composure starts to strip itself away. They'll maybe cross their arms with that twitchy, shaky, tension, or they'll grab down little wheezes of embarrassed air, or they'll simply hood their face under their palm, trying to hide how fast they're slipping: how fast *we're* slipping, because I'll be weakening with them by then, I'll be just as lost, pulled equally tight against the moment when we both stop caring and let it disgrace us—when we laugh.

I'm sombre though, this morning: on my own and therefore less likely to go astray.

The man with the 50s suit and the heavy glasses, he notices me frowning and nods, understanding of a grief that I don't have, because there is no real reason for me to be here. I met the deceased perhaps five times: each one completely unremarkable. He is no more to me than a lanky, softly variable recollection, the after-image of a friend of friends. He will have had qualities, I'm sure, but I don't know them.

Over by the door, the taller woman with the reddish hair— I think she's the sister—she hinges forward and catches at a teenage boy, hugs him in viciously while she faces something unknowable over his head, robbed eyes still fighting, puzzling. She ought to be somewhere more dignified than this. The cemetery outside seems all but abandoned and, inside, decades of cheap, municipal gloss have drowned out the contours of each moulding, every window frame; there's nothing for her to see that isn't faintly grubby and miserable with soaked-in nicotine.

In fact, being in this building is depressing, which is tautological—the people you'd expect to come here will already *be* depressed.

Me, I'm quite chipper, personally, but I would prefer it to be much easier for me to stay that way.

So I worry through the murmuring clusters and out to the corridor where I end up studying, once again, the tiny black pin board on which today's schedule is unevenly displayed, the white plastic letters fixed into a list of surnames and starting times—

the current gathering is second out of six. And although every-body possible has surely already arrived, there are still fifteen minutes left to wait. We all, for our various reasons, have turned up too soon and the room behind me is now unsteady—even I can feel—with the concentration of involuntary hope, a habit nobody has shaken yet: the one that expects a final, impossible guest.

I need some space.

My breath is visible, even before I step completely beyond the front doors. They are awkwardly stiff and really must trouble the progress of pall-bearers, or biers. That's what I'd guess: I have no intention of loitering until the hearse pulls up just to prove myself right. Me there: a stranger waiting on the doorstep: it would look odd. The whole facility, anyway, is plainly not funeral-friendly, there's no need for additional evidence. Serve them right, if people start making their own arrangements: dumping off their relatives in rivers, or allotments, or the more accessible beauty-spots.

It's not in good taste to think so, I realise that. But then it's not exactly tasteful to add inconvenience to pre-existing grief—if anyone's being insensitive, it's not me. I should complain. I should write a letter to the relevant authority.

The driveway's shameful, too: all pitted. I have to be quite careful where I walk. And I mustn't consider the fine particulates, the vapours, drifting down from the grey, unsubtle smoke-stack: gathering in potholes, frozen puddles.

Out under the open, I clap my hands together for the sake of warmth and causing a disturbance, showing proof of life, and then I regret it—too loud. A single blackbird flicks over the grass, its little chips of alarm disappearing, muffled in the frost. I could head back to my car and leave this. No one would notice my absence. I'm not needed.

Which is, perhaps, what will make me stay.

To ease the minutes by, I pace out a slow, wide circle over the grass, set an ice dust melting on my shoes. When I pause first, I can see a small disturbance of colour, reddish flowers propped against a stone. Another pause, and I can watch the white depth of new mist unpicking the detail from the trees. Another, and I could see the car park if I felt so inclined, but I do not—there's nothing in it for me.

Back indoors, then: I might as well.

Yes, I might as well go back indoors. I do have other options, but I have no need to choose them, since I'm already here.

God, look at the place—it's inexcusable.

Sometimes I wish that my mind would, for once, stop talking, stop telling me what to do.

Back indoors it is, though. Why not. Up the steps, a strong tug, and then through.

And, at once, I can feel the difference, I can tell—I'd hoped this wouldn't happen and I'd hoped it would, and now, whatever my wishes, it has—Paul's here.

I haven't seen him, but I know: while I was walking and not thinking of him and not searching out his car: while I wasn't looking, in he came. Same as ever, without my permission, in he came.

He has no more excuse for attending than I do. We swapped pleasantries with the dead man together, just those four or five times: we neither of us ever knew his birthday, or his middle initial, or if he enjoyed his job—if he *had* a job. We're here for each other, to do ourselves harm.

Which would, of course, hardly matter, if we hadn't once been kind, better than kind.

I mean, I can no longer remember when I first realised that I could tell where Paul was without looking, without being told. Maybe it's a scent thing, like moths finding each other, or turtles—turtles can smell their home from miles away. At the start it was only good: easing through doorways and drawing in while all I could touch was his touch: in the nudge of other bodies, the curves of forward motion on my skin, the warm lean of the walls towards me, the shifts of my mind: everything, him.

This morning is still much the same, reality turning seasick and raw, but when we meet we'll give each other nothing but offence.

I step into the side room, anyway: deeper and deeper: and find, by himself beside the empty fireplace, the man that I used to agree with and who used to agree with me.

Paul's expecting me, that's obvious—his back turned pre-emptively away from the open door, his shoulders wary. I think he's gained weight, only a little. The trousers I've never seen before, but that's a jacket I was very used to—for some reason seeing it hurts—and it won't keep him warm enough, not today, it isn't practical. Slip your arm inside it, though, and there will be heat, held close at the small of his back. It was something worth finding, I remember that.

His hands: something else I remember. Even across this distance, they're changing the space between my fingers, making it ache. He's fussing in and out of his pockets and, if he's shaking, I'm not close enough to tell. I'm also unwilling to look down at my own hands. We do both tremble too easily and this will be much harder if either of us seems moved, or weak.

I would like to pay no attention to his head, the back of his head, his hair. I'd say that he's just had it cut. I'd say that I have the feel of it, singing in my palm like the ghost of some old injury.

Then, walking between us, comes that man with the heavy glasses again, which he now removes softly and rubs with the end of his tie. Next, he peers about and shows the room how the frame has impressed little grooves in the bridge of his nose and the flesh at his temples.

Must be too tight. Or maybe his eyesight's perfect, but he had to buy some glasses to fit his grooves.

A year ago, if I hadn't said it, then Paul would—that's the way we're made. It wouldn't have been meant unpleasantly: the thoughts occurred and we allowed them and they were ours. They only seem unpleasant to think without company.

The man slips back into his glasses and moves on and, before I can be ready, Paul moves too, swings round gingerly, as if his body has become uncooperative now, or unsafe. Then, with a yard or so left between us, we both stop and I was expecting this, but still it catches me like a slap: his expression of vehement weariness and contempt, there just for me. Under it, are the traces of what he can't control: there in the mouth, the eyes, the honest places: his absolute anger, his fear, his pain.

And I am quite aware, believe me, that I'm presenting exactly the same kind of face to him.

He breaks off and goes to sit, hunched forward, his elbows leaning on his knees, head dropped. Anyone who saw him might imagine he's exhausted, or upset. Anyone who cared about him would slip over there quietly and stroke his back, or cup his forehead, kneel beside him with their hand braced on his thigh while they asked after his problem and said what they could to make it fade. Anyone who cared.

He ducks up slightly, shading his eyes with spread fingers, peering out at me like a boy and then flinching when I look at him, withdrawing again. Which is perfectly natural, because I'm his problem: there is nothing I can do to help him, other than ceasing to be.

And I'm not entirely sure I want to help. Why should I stop him hurting when he won't stop hurting me.

It went wrong, that's all, completely wrong. First we laughed at strangers and then, being so happy and so much at ease, we laughed at each other and proved we were safe in our hands, because we didn't mean a word. But then a little jab would meet a jab and a cut would meet a cut and we'd apologise and there would be tenderness, but the kind you only feel when there's a bruise. None of it was intended: no one was really attacking, we were both just defending ourselves.

But we didn't stop. So now we are this: each of us a bad mirror for the other. Not anything better, not anything softer, not anything to do with love.

Naturally, I can't say this, because I won't speak to him, because he won't speak to me and vice versa.

I'm getting an angry headache, possibly a migraine. He's my sole trigger for the migraines, I never used to have them before. The stomach cramps, the dreams, the shortened attention span: in a purely pathological way, he's much more a part of me these days than he ever was.

At no signal of which I'm aware, the groups around me start to slide, conversations ending, and the whole crowd shuffling and bumping towards the door.

I won't go out with them, I can't face it. Once they're all in their seats and the music's started, I'm going home: I find I'm too tired for anything else. I walk to face the only window, stare into the pale day, while the room at my back empties, becomes still.

I know that he hasn't left, either: I don't have to turn and see. He's sitting behind me, just as he was, his breath now audible in the quiet—I can hear mine, too.

Our situation is ridiculous, laughable, and I want to be able to laugh. The fact that I can't is, in itself, quite funny, if I think about it: quite bizarre that I can lose my own nature so easily, just because he's with me. And it really should be very amusing that this will go on, that I have nothing better, that no matter what, I still want to be sure that we won't leave each other alone.

A Bad Son

Ronald was holding on.

He was managing: riding it, doing something dangerous, doing something he couldn't do. Very softly and wonderfully, he began to think this ought to mean that he was being someone new. The ground was snarling past beneath him and close by his sides and this wasn't pretending and wasn't wishing—because neither of those worked—but he was really here with nothing gone wrong yet, not even something small—so he must be someone else now—better than he was—maybe changed just this minute, maybe by miracle.

His father said that miracles don't happen and his mother said it, too. They could be wrong though, he saw that: because he was holding on.

He remembered his feet, he was meant to be braking with his feet, jamming his heels down in the snow, but he didn't want to, didn't honestly understand how, and going this fast was good, anyway, this suited him fine, the jars and bangs hitting so close to each other, they almost became the one thing and made it hard for him to think, which was what he wanted—the less he could hear in his head, the more he liked it. Soon he'd find just the right speed where he'd stop having any words inside him, or any people, or bits of things he'd seen: he would reach the racing speed that could empty him out of everyone. He could feel it beginning to take him, to make him clean.

Ronald shut his eyes and let himself slip and be part of a big, long shine and he smiled and smiled and stretched back so that he was lying down, resting on it, the way that another boy might, one who did this all the time. He'd been scared before he started, but you could only be scared for a while and then it changed— became something else—this time it had burst to nothing, to a hot, white light that was marvellous and still and he was so happy with it that he let the day take his breath.

Before it kicked and tipped away beneath him, yanked his legs, the rest of him following sharper than he'd thought it could, plunging while he imagined smearing, being rubbed out, replaced.

Then something massive caught him, lifted him up.

And he was going to look and see what it was like to be in flight when some other thing wrapped around him, springing and cold and mainly soft, but with scratches in it.

When it let him go, he knew he would drop.

He landed on his back.

Very close to his face, it seemed, there was the sky, a sore blue, but peaceful, and he was breathing again—a lot—in and out so much that it burned when he swallowed. Ronald moved cautiously and the snow creaked in reply. He thought of things he could have broken, or how easily he might have banged his head, or bitten off his tongue—which would be awful, that would mean you couldn't speak—but when he shifted, patted, he discovered nothing much that hurt, besides his throat. He was probably all right.

He was going to try standing when he heard Jim whoop and yell, crashing towards him, down between the trees, and laughing. This would be OK, though. Jim wasn't going to make fun of him: he didn't think so, anyway.

Full of a beautiful calmness, Ronald sat up and considered the pine tree in front of him—the one that had brought him to his stop—it looked enormous, as if you couldn't hit it and live. The overturned sledge was beside him, crossing the last, dark swing of its tracks, and over his legs was the mess of slush and needles he must have knocked loose when he crashed. Then Jim was here and was hammering on his back and hat—not too hard, only friendly.

"How're you laughing, tumshie?"

Ronald shut his mouth and the laughing stopped. He hadn't realised it was him making all that noise.

"Eh? You're mad. Right intae it." Jim marched forward and brushed the new scar on the pine's trunk respectfully. He glanced back and grinned. "Playing chicken with a tree. Mad."

Ronald felt his mouth become uneasy. "But I didn't break the sledge? Did I?"

Jim kicked one of its runners, unconcerned, "That? No. We slid that off the top of the barn to test it, like? Fucking indestructible." It sounded OK when Jim swore—or when Ronald's father started: getting angry with Barbara Castle, or because of the Icelanders stealing British cod, or when a thing went wrong, even something small, and made him shout. They were people who could handle the words—they never sounded stupid and as if they were pretending, not the way Ronald did.

Trying to think of a word he'd be able to say, Ronald struggled his legs in under himself until he could kneel and dig at the snow and yank up the sledge's tow rope.

"You're wanting another shot?" Jim sounded slightly impressed, but Ronald didn't truly want to do anything, except to get warm again, maybe. He hadn't expected to be mad, or to stay on, even: everything had been an accident. It had been easier to try the sledge than admit he'd never sat on one before, that was all.

Jim peered back at the slope professionally, "Even Billy hasna came thon way . . ."

Ronald stood, tipped his head far back to take in the whole trail he'd left, and then had to shake his gaze away again—the slope didn't look possible, it was far too steep and had rocks: bare, black rocks: dodging out from the snow. He almost started to be frightened, but then remembered he was meant to be new—he was the boy who'd ridden down with no trouble and, better than that, Jim knew he'd done it—he'd been brave with a witness to see. Ronald tried stretching up his fists, as if he'd scored a goal, but it went wrong and felt silly, so he wagged his arms and stamped his feet and made a war dance out of it. He howled a bit—the howling made him happy. He'd been brave and Jim had seen it.

"Fucking Mad Ronnie. Mad as fuck." Jim punched his arm and Ronald slapped at him in return without thinking, but that must have been the right thing to do, because Jim just took the rope from him and said, "No, I'll pull it home—no more time for anything today, or the old dear'll kill us." He paused. "Better no tell her, eh?"

Ronald was happy to agree, "Yes, better not." He was good at secrets.

Again Jim punched him, this time on the shoulder: "And you'll be needing a rest." He started walking, the sledge following with a flip and a bounce, after no more than a moment of unwillingness: Jim was strong.

"Aye." Ronald always said *yes* at home, but Jim wouldn't know that. "Aye. Mad as fuck," which didn't sound as shy as it could have. He started off, too, determined he would keep up this time and not have to pretend he was stopping to look at things, so that he could rest. There was melt water down his wellingtons—Jim's wellingtons, actually—and some had run in from his collar, as far as his back, but the damp was getting warm, so he needn't worry.

"*Ronnie, Ronnie, madasfuck, madasfuck, madasfuck. Ronnie, Ronnie madasfuck. Mad. As. Fuck.*" Jim made up songs about everyone, always to the same tune, and then just sang them—he didn't care if people heard, or if they got angry.

Ronald trotted on until he was level with Jim—possibly ahead—even though it made his thighs sting. When the song, his song, started for the second time he joined in, careful to control his breathing and not pant. The rhythm helped him move faster and let him think of being in an army and marching and shouting with people he was like. Comrades, that's what you called it—being comrades.

Their singing knocked every crow up out of the little wood; just the two of them, they'd shouted that loud. And, because of the snow, Ronald could tell nobody but them had been here for days—not a mark to spoil it, except where they'd walked. No one was near, either, not anywhere he looked. They were the only things moving, so this was their own. He was the only one who noticed, so this was his.

Ronald pushed out a short run forward, the afternoon spinning in him, being light again, brighter and brighter, being good. He let himself fall in the snow, face up and still singing. *Ronnie, Ronnie . . .*

"Now what?"

"*Madasfuck*—Leave me here." Ronald said this quietly, because suddenly it was needed, what should be.

"What?"

He did want to stay. "Leave me." If this was his, it would take him away, what was left of how he'd been, and he could disappear.

"Oh." Jim made a trial drop of snow on to Ronald's chest. "Leave you? Have to be camouflaged if I leave you . . ." He gathered a larger scoop and threw it at Ronald's throat—some went in his mouth.

It tasted of being invisible. "That's OK." Ronald reminded himself that he needn't be scared, he didn't have to any more. He could be brand new, could be mad as fuck.

He thought of the yogis who had themselves buried for weeks in India—they only breathed once a day, or something, and because of that they were fine when their followers came back and dug them up. You could do whatever you wanted, if you could concentrate enough: walk on coals and levitate, breathe in one nostril and out the other—hot, cold, beds of nails: you didn't have to feel a thing.

And under snow there'd be no feeling and only the whiteness in your head, no sounds. Better than the sledge—it wouldn't stop.

Jim had found a rhythm and was scraping snow over him now from either side in flat armfuls. Not wanting to spoil it, Ronald raised his head only slowly and saw he was almost covered. In a while, you wouldn't tell him from anything else.

"No, you've got to stay flat, mind."

"My face?"

Jim paused while the idea of this caught between them— Ronald pushing what they would do, volunteering to be buried properly. "Your face? Well, aye."

Surprisingly gently, Jim built a rim of snow up around Ronald's head, patting it solid. Ronald listened to his ears being stopped with the grind of close movement and the gathering pace of his breath. Then the cold was pressed in at his cheeks, his chin, his mouth, and was closed down from his forehead.

If you died of cold it was nice, he'd read that. You went sleepy and then you slept and then didn't wake.

His face was throbbing, the chill aching in his teeth, but he let that happen and ignored it. He stared at the sky, weaving his eyes, focusing on how free they were, and how odd and bare it seemed to look at things. Bits of him were burning, somehow, and this might fix the change in him, truly make him another person.

Leaning over and blocking the view, Jim shouted, "I'm away then." He sounded partly lonely. Ronald's side read the pressure of his boots as he walked past.

Then it was Ronald alone, and trying to find he was someone else—getting strong.

It was quiet outside him, all dumb. He didn't know if his ears still worked: they hurt a lot. His lips and forehead, too. Inside, he was still noisy, having to think.

He wasn't a yogi, Ronald realised, he wasn't anything yet. There was nothing in him that seemed important. Lying in the cold this way was making him shrink to the point where he might not matter any more. It wasn't what he'd hoped for, wasn't fair.

But it wouldn't be bad to get sleepy and sleep. That wouldn't be the worst.

He would miss his mother, that was the only thing. He thought she would miss him. They did things together whenever they could, when nothing had gone wrong. But maybe that didn't matter, either.

Ronald waited for the cold to stop him feeling, scrub everything. He waited to make a miracle.

Even though a miracle you made yourself might not count.

If you didn't matter—there was a dark, red pain near his eyes—if you didn't matter—he almost understood—if you didn't matter, then nothing did. If nothing mattered, then you wouldn't care. You could do anything and not care.

He wanted that. It would be the best. It would be Ronald, mad as fuck.

Ronald tilted his head back to laugh. A trickle of water ran down into his nose and then quick, to the back of his throat, made him splutter up, heaving clear into the air again.

He coughed, rubbed his face and started it tingling, coughed again, doubled over, and then made a point of spitting. Jim probably spat whenever he wanted to, was good at it.

Yes, but he could be good at it, too. He could learn.

"Hey! Wait, though!"

Up ahead, Jim was tiny.

"Hey! Hey, I'm coming!"

He'd lasted longer than he'd thought—Jim far ahead, trudging and kicking at snow.

"Hey!"

He'd lasted a mad, long time. Mad as fuck. You could do anything, like that.

Ronald staggered forward, then attempted a trot, a wallowing run.

"Hey! Jim!"

This time, Jim span round and opened his arms, yelled for him. "*Yes!* And Mad Ronnie bounces back."

Ronald pushed harder at that, bolted, the skin near his lips stinging.

He arrived, almost certain that he was worth a celebration, and risked a punch at Jim's body. "Uh hu. Mad Ronnie." He was out of breath, but boiling with success, his joints easy, his arms and legs belonging to Mad Ronnie now—someone who was used to passing tests and having victories. "Uh hu. That's me."

"Good thing, as well. Couldn't think what I'd say to the old dear—you not with me and that—she'd have gone mental . . ." Jim wasn't afraid of anyone except his mother. "And we're late—come on and tank it, eh?"

Before Ronald could think, they did both begin racing: tripping and slithering, battering into each other and then stumbling on. The evening had sunk in at them quickly, a short dash of pink light and then the start of dark, and the farm's lights showing clearly, spilling in yellow glows as they pulled towards it. By this time, Ronald was nothing but muscles and lungs and the hot clout of his heart and the knowledge that he'd had a great day, the best day. He hadn't made one mistake.

Although they were both cautious around her, Jim's mother was in a good mood when she saw them: scolding, but not seriously. "Oh, for goodness' sake, Jim, what were you trying to do—drown him?" Ronald stood close to Jim in the cake-smelling kitchen, feet and fingers seeming swollen in the violent warmth. Mrs. Dickson half smiled. "Look at him—he's soaked."

Ronald hadn't met her very often, but was used to her speaking about him as if he were a small and unusual machine that Jim was bound to break. "I'm OK, though, Mrs. Dickson." To be respectful, he talked to her in his classroom voice—more Scottish than his home voice, but not as Scottish as his playtime one and not loud and with possible swearing the way he might always be now when he thought that he wanted to. "It was the snow." The words were awkward: his changes from one thing to another didn't always work straight away.

"Snow doesn't jump over boys by itself. Take off everything that's wet." She made her voice harder—the way people did for family things when they wanted no arguments. "Jim will carry them to the drier and will lend you his dressing gown. The blue one, Jim. On you go."

Mrs. Dickson wasn't pretty, so Ronald tried to be as nice as he could to her, because ugly people were sad the whole time and that was the worst thing in the world.

"Yes, Mrs. Dickson."

"Don't *yes*—just go away, the pair of you—you're dripping everywhere."

"Yes, Mrs. Dickson."

Upstairs in Jim's room, Ronald sat on the end of the bed in his vest and pants—these were slightly wet, too, but he wasn't going to take them off. The dressing gown was waiting next to him: but it seemed funny to wear someone else's clothes, and he didn't need it yet, he was fine.

The noises of a strange house rose up to him and he tried to make sense of them. Ronald could hear, he thought, all the televisions playing at once: they sounded like people fighting, but they were only televisions, he could be sure: talking and playing music, in the way they were meant to do. And there was some kind of motor running, further below.

The place was a terrible mess: his mother would never let things be that way at home, she would know better. Here, the only neat places were the kitchen and the best lounge. Still, the house was much bigger than where he lived and it had all those televisions—three—and a snooker table and a monster freezer full of hamburgers and chickens and half a lamb—he'd gone with Jim and looked—and they had a weird, huge stove here that Jim was allowed to cut wood for: the small bits, anyway. He supposed that the Dicksons must be rich: they just didn't seem like rich people when you met them.

On his birthday watch it was nearly five o'clock, so at home his mother might be starting to get dinner ready. She might be making a cup of tea for herself before everything had to go on, that's what he would guess. If he was there and it was all right, he would have milk with her in his glass, the two of them resting and getting peace, like you sometimes needed to. He must have to go soon.

He decided to put on the dressing gown, after all. It wasn't a bad one, cosy: it smelt of different washing and the Dicksons: and Ronald wanted to curl up on his side in it for a while. Curling helped you to be comfortable and quiet: his mother had explained that to him. It was something that you only did at home, though, not with other people.

He pulled his arms up inside their borrowed sleeves until even his fingers were gone. It would be awful to have no hands. Ronald started to picture how he'd lose them both at once, maybe fighting off a dog, or something like that, maybe if he tried to stop somebody being hurt. Jim sneaked in without him noticing.

"Ha! Dreaming!" Jim pounced him flat on the bed and they rolled together, Ronald wondering how much he ought to struggle, before Jim leaped away again and stood. "Come on and I'll show you something. Something mad as fuck, ken?"

"I, yes . . . Aye." While Jim rummaged under the bed, Ronald licked the inside of his top lip—he must have banged it, because now it tasted hot and was beginning to be thicker than it should be. He could trace the faint imprint of his teeth. This didn't trouble him, though—he needn't think about it, not if he didn't decide to.

"Here now." Jim emerged with his schoolbag and held it up—which wasn't that mad, really, but Ronald kept watching, anyway.

"Just what we need." Jim bounded across to the window and turned the bag upside down, shook it empty and then looked over. Ronald could tell he was asking for a nod, or an *aye*, or just a shrug, perhaps, and that would be enough to make him start. Jim was going to do something awful, but it was going to be Ronald's fault. And Ronald knew this shouldn't matter, because nothing could, so he didn't stop his head from drooping forward and then he smiled and made Jim fling up the window, jam it wide, and let the night fall in.

Ronald's stomach twisted, but nicely: not like being scared, like badness climbing in to help him have fun.

Before the first cold could come and touch them, Jim lifted

a slim, blue book: his homework register, the one you were never, ever allowed to lose: and then skimmed it sideways, far outside. They heard it drop in the snow—a faint, unforgivable landing. Jim picked a jotter next and it went the same way, between the snow gleam and the deep sky.

This time the word rose behind Ronald's teeth and fitted perfectly, "Fuck."

"Want a shot?" Jim offered the hard-backed grammar book they had to use: hundreds of pointless sentences inside it, each one built from mysterious pieces—verbs and nouns and punctuation marks. They didn't matter at all.

Ronald knew that Jim would get in trouble, that the snow would ruin his books and that everyone who could was going to give him a row, at least a row. But then Ronald was taking the book and holding it and understanding what a fine thing it would be to kill it, drown it in snow, and Jim was being keen, straight at him, and believing that he was Mad Ronnie and that this would be something to please him—Jim was there, wanting to please him and keep up—when none of the boys like Jim had ever wanted that before.

And it wasn't Ronald's book, so it wouldn't matter. He could be bad and it wouldn't matter, not for him.

He leaned to look out of the window and saw, clear in the sparking, rolling white, the small dark patch that marked where the water was kept free at one edge of the frozen pond. Jim's father had set a hose that ran water there and stopped the ice from closing to let his ducks go out and have a swim. The ducks were a rare breed, expensive.

The pond would be the place: the best, worst place. Anything that went in there would just disappear. It was a long way, but Ronnie could throw, he knew how to do that. At home, he would practise for hours in the garden, concentrating, imagining he was aiming at a face.

So now he dipped his eyelids and breathed in the way that an Indian yogi would. He fixed where the pond was and sort of stretched towards it in his mind, set a figure there, standing, helpless for him to hit. And then he curved back the whole of his arm. He breathed out. He flicked from his shoulder, along to his wrist. He meant it.

Then he opened his eyes and, along with Jim, watched the book spin across the light from the farmhouse windows. There was something beautiful about it, the shimmer of its edges, the clean flight. He couldn't really see the last part of its journey, but then a final splash came and

"Fuck." Jim studied him, solemn, and handed him a jotter, taking another for himself, letting Ronald help to ruin him.

The two of them threw together after that, fast and faster, whispering between their teeth and hearing and liking the impact of every book. And the ruler, the pencils, the rubber, the pencil case: all of them vanished in water and snow. Ronald was sure that he never missed the pond.

Nothing left to throw, they stood, leaning out, their breath drifting in hot clouds ahead of them, Ronald with the idea that everywhere around him was their secret now and a proof of who he was.

"Shut that bloody window. D'you want the flu?"

Jim's father, enormous in the doorway, making them bump together when they flinched, Ronald's stomach kicking, but "Ronnie—that's your father on the telephone" was all that came next, so it must be OK—there was only a problem about the window, which Jim was shuddering down—they weren't going to get into trouble for anything else.

Ronald half sprinted out under Mr. Dickson's outstretched arm. "Easy now—the one down the stairs in the hall."

And, after that, things got difficult, because Ronald was excited, was having this fantastic time, was getting strong, and his dad said that he could stay—there was no need to come home, because tomorrow was a Sunday and the Dicksons didn't mind—he could have dinner with them and sleep in their house and still be with Jim in the morning and get picked up later and it would be fun. He could stay away.

"Could I?"

"If you want."

Ronald couldn't help it—he did want. Somewhere, he had this worry about staying: it pressed at the edge of his happiness, trying to get through: but, when he concentrated, it weakened, sank.

"Please, if I could, then. Yes."

"All right."

Easily done—then the run to Jim after and not feeling guilty, not feeling a thing, not even about the books.

Dinner with another whole family was awkward. The heat from Ronald's newly dried clothes didn't seem to have left them and by the end of the soup he felt sticky and small.

"So what do you think of the oil then, Ronnie? North Sea's full of it, they say. Fancy a job on a rig, will you? There'll be plenty by the time you're ready."

It was hard to tell if Mr. Dickson was joking. He never asked questions that made any sense—but the way that he said them made you think they should and that probably you were stupid. "I . . . I don't . . ." Ronnie was blushing, Jim's two older brothers watching him like sheep-dogs and making it worse. "I can't swim."

"All the better. Canna swim in the North Sea, son—too cold. You'd be glad to drown quick there."

Mrs. Dickson sucked in air between her teeth and Ronnie saw this make her husband frown.

"Bloody Yanks . . ." Mr. Dickson steered the subject slightly to one side: "Out of Vietnam and into Aberdeen. We'll not see a penny, I doubt—it'll all go back to Texas wi' our oil." Another suck of teeth came and Ronald ducked his head, not wanting the fight to start while he was here.

Mr. Dickson halted, stabbed at his chops, but then smiled. Mrs. Dickson nodded, satisfied, and Ronald's scalp relaxed. Mr. Dickson rubbed his stubbly chin—he didn't ever get a beard, but was never clean-shaven, either. Ronald's father shaved each morning: whatever happened, however late he'd been awake—he kept tidy. And he didn't ask Ronald about what he wanted to do.

"Well, I'll tell you anyway, Ronnie, dinna be a fairmer." The Dickson menfolk panted quietly with laughter at the thought of this—of Farmer Ronnie—while Mrs. Dickson pursed her lips and Ronald blushed harder, until Jim pinched him under the table, then winked when he turned to see why—*we know who you are, though: Mad Ronnie: the two of us, book murderers, we know.* Then Ronald started to laugh himself and dug in to finish his chop. Even though they had bones, Ronald liked chops.

The table eased then, and people told jokes that nobody minded and the pudding was chocolate cake and custard, which Ronald also really liked—his mother bought puddings now, she didn't make them any more. Jim began to tell the story of the sledging, taking the risk of saying what they'd done, making everything that happened seem exciting and on purpose. One of the cats had slipped in and rubbed around Ronald's shins, being friendly, so he tried to concentrate mostly on that, but still sweated inside the worst blushes yet.

A proper yogi wouldn't have that problem and neither would Mad Ronnie: he'd been happy with all this. Ronald, though, couldn't prevent the narrow slip of thought that he ought to be at home, that choosing to stay here had been a mistake.

"Look at you—you're half asleep." Mrs. Dickson leaned to squeeze his shoulder and gave him a soft, unsteady feeling. "That's what you get for trying to break your neck all afternoon. We'll put you in a bath and then it's bed." She *was* much uglier than his mother, but had comfortable eyes. He couldn't imagine her crying.

"Yes, Mrs. Dickson."

But then she squeezed again and looked at him as if he'd made her sad: "You're a wee soul." He hadn't meant to upset her.

Mr. Dickson cleared his throat and came in loud, brisk, "He's a grand lad—polite. First time we've had one of them here."

Everyone smiled towards Ronald, but apart from Jim, every one of them looked as if they'd seen something in him that was unhappy, or maybe frightening. His head started to get tight.

The bath didn't make him feel better: the soap wrong and odd-smelling and the towels scratchy. He got back into Jim's dressing gown and walked into the cool of the corridor holding his folded clothes, pants hidden in the middle, and with a swimming feeling against his eyes. He thought he might be sick, but Mrs. Dickson was there waiting for him so he tried to look fine.

"Oh, you are tired." She led him away from Jim's room. "Which is a good thing." The dressing gown straggled on the floor as he walked, as if he was very little. She kept talking, "We don't want any riots in the night—we're up at five, so we need our sleep," and then opened a new door, let him edge into an empty sort of bedroom, everything brown, with a huge bed in it and a chair, nothing else. "But if you need anything, you come and say so—we'll be in there." She pointed, Ronald supposed, at another room somewhere along the hall where she might stay at night with Mr. Dickson, but he didn't pay any attention. He wasn't ever going to go and wake them up.

"Good-night then, Ronnie." She kissed the top of his head, which he hadn't expected. He couldn't imagine her kissing Jim—unless she did it when no one else was there.

"Good night, Mrs. Dickson."

It was a relief when she closed his door, because then he could leave his things on the chair, turn off the light, get into the bed and curl—that would mean he got peace.

The mattress made hollow, metal noises as he climbed in, the blankets heavy over him. He didn't have pyjamas, but hadn't liked to say. It would be OK, though—yogis never had them. Air scuttled in the radiator. Then he was by himself without a sound and there was nothing left to stop him knowing.

I made a mistake—a bad mistake—I shouldn't have wanted to stay away—I shouldn't have asked to.

It wasn't my fault, though—it was theirs. I wanted to be away—not for a long time—just for a day—a quiet day.

It wasn't my fault.

She's there now, on her own.

His mother—with her best necklace of the red beads which were garnets and from his grandmother who was dead before he was born. His mother's eyes—blue like his eyes, unless she was crying—and her smell, her warm, home smell—and the way she was the only one who called him Ronald so that was his name, his real name—and how she kissed him sometimes, on his eyes and then his mouth, which was the best—and the way she danced to the radio and made you not want to join in, only watch, because she was so happy, and you could just face her and breathe in being so happy and that was enough—and her hands, they were the nicest hands—and he'd left her alone. She was there with his father and no one to help and you couldn't trust him. Ronald understood that and she didn't, not until after. She was on her own there and something bad would be happening.

Please make her safe.

Fuck.

It was part of his head now, his word, the way it was his father's.

Fuck.

Please make her safe.

He couldn't ask the Dicksons to let him telephone, because he couldn't tell them why. Anyway, if he did call, then his father would answer and lie, the way he always lied, and wouldn't come to fetch him, not tonight.

We could run away, stay somewhere else together, stay with the Dicksons, or anywhere. We could run. I know how to do it, I know what we'd take.

Ronald wasn't strong—he couldn't break the door when his father locked it—Ronald couldn't hit him, not enough. When he shouted sometimes, inhaled like a yogi, full into his chest until it hurt and then screamed out and kept on, kept on until he couldn't hear it but it was there, like somebody holding him in the throat—sometimes then his father would stop. He would stare hard at Ronald, but then he would leave, drive somewhere and not come back until it was morning. Ronald could make him go, but he always came back.

If she went with me, we'd be us together, we'd be all right. She should let me take her. She should fucking let me.

"Hey, Ronnie . . ."

Jim closed the door and bare-footed softly to the bed.

"Hey, Ronnie."

Ronald swallowed and his voice came out tiny. "Yes." The sheet tightened across him as Jim sat on the bed.

"The books—they'll be fucked, eh? No use." Jim sniffed.

"Uh hu."

"I thought so."

The dark, quiet nudged in at them. Jim sniffed again, "Mrs. Jepson hates me—fucking cow."

This was the way things went. Ronald would like someone and then he'd make them sad. He never was able to hurt anyone he hated. His badness never came to him at the right time.

He tried to be friendly for Jim, now the damage was done. "She can't hate you—teachers aren't allowed."

"She fucking does. And I'll no have any books on Monday. No homework."

"Say you lost them."

"All of them?"

"Aye."

"She'll think I'm at it. She'll tell the old dear."

Ronald couldn't manage another lie. "Probably."

"I'm fucked."

Jim lay back, maybe crying—Ronald hadn't thought he could and wanted to be sad with him, but it didn't work. He'd wanted to cry when he thought of his mother, but hadn't been able to then, either. There was something wrong with him. "You could tell Mrs. Jepson I helped . . ." He didn't completely mean this, but he ought to be in trouble for something: he would deserve it.

Jim let him get away with just the offer. "She'd never believe that. You don't do anything." He sounded better now, but a bit angry.

"I do things . . . I do. She just doesn't notice."

"If I told her you'd helped, she'd have an eppie—at me." Jim stopped. There were sputtering noises, little giggling shakes of the bed, "How's this—I could give her a heart attack. I could tell her I'd thrown all the fucking books out the fucking window and didn't care, tell her to fuck herself—she'd *fucking die*." He snorted a muffled laugh. "How would that be, eh?" Jim didn't stay sad long, not ever.

Ronald thought Mrs. Jepson was nice. "I don't know . . ." She let him stay late and help her tidy things.

"Ach, I don't care. I'll be on the farm, working, as soon as I'm sixteen. Or I could join the army—the paras, eh? Out the back of a plane, wherever you like."

Ronald pictured the books flying, the beautiful skim of them, the feel of the badness when it belonged to him. "It was good, throwing them. Wasn't it."

"Too right." Jim stretched. "It was Mad Ronnie, that. Mad Ronnie." He lay still and then began to grunt, almost snoring.

At first Ronald thought he was pretending to be asleep, "Jim," but then his breathing drifted, "Jim," and he'd gone.

So the touch of the house he'd escaped snapped shut against Ronald, came and claimed him, and he wasn't Mad Ronnie any more, was only himself and couldn't fight it.

Fuck her. **Fuck her.**

We don't have to stay, we can't have to stay.

He *should* love her. He *did* love her. She maybe didn't love him.

Fuck.

Because he was a fucking bastard like his father.

Please make her safe. It matters that she's safe.

He lay still the way he did under the snow. He wouldn't wake Jim.

Please, if you make her be safe, I'll not go away again. I'll always stay. Please make her safe. Don't let her think I ran away. Don't let her be lonely.

But, after a time, Jim woke up anyway: stirred, slid down from the bed and left without speaking. Ronald didn't notice him that much.

Please make her safe.

Fuck.

Fuck.

Please make me not feel a thing.

It was the same way at home when the shouting started, and the other noise, when everything ran in his head and dragged him on, too fast.

Please make her fucking safe please make her safe pleasemakeherfuckingsafepleasemake hersafe please.

Please fucking make me not feel a thing not feel a thing

It would last until morning, because he hadn't changed.

not feel a thing

Breakfast was in the kitchen, but he didn't want it. His mouth tasted funny—he hadn't brushed his teeth last night—no toothbrush.

"You all right?" Jim was folding bacon between two slices of toast. They were there by themselves, everyone else out working.

"Uh hu."

"No hungry?"

"Didn't sleep."

"Oh." Jim took a mouthful of his sandwich. "Good that you stayed, ken. You could come back and stay again, eh no?"

No. I can't ever. "Aye." Ronald could tell he might cry and stumbled up to get more orange juice.

"You're thirsty." Jim was different this morning, more careful, more the same size as Ronald.

"Aye."

They finished in silence and went out into the snow, the hard cold making Ronald cough.

"What you want to do?" Jim anxious for Mad Ronnie to have an idea.

"I don't know. I'm not sure when my dad's coming—he'll pick me up."

"After lunch."

"Maybe not as late as that."

"No, maybe—that would be right." Jim kicked at a tyre rut. "Folk don't come out here much—they think it'll be boring."

Over to their left, the corner of a jotter was visible. They turned to face away from it.

"I'll say it isn't boring."

"Will you?"

"Aye." And Ronald mashed together a snowball, aimed it at a sapling, a thin one, felt the way it would fly and let it go. He hit.

Jim didn't sound cheerful, was not like himself. "That's it. That's what we can do. Target practice. Aye . . . That's what."

So they trudged round the house and threw snowballs, quietly thumping snow over every sign of a book that showed. There was no point: when a thaw came, they'd be found. Jim would be there to take the blame and he wouldn't.

Ronald could tell they were both uneasy and it *was* boring, but mainly he'd already left, was thinking about being on his way, getting taken home.

"So, *fuck you!*"

Ronald slammed his last snowball into the side of Jim's head. Jim breathed out for a moment, blank-faced, possibly dangerous.

Then he scrambled for new snow, laughing, and hurled back a lump of wet cold. "Right in the fucking puss. Like that, eh?"

Ronald forced a laugh of his own, made it louder, rushed his arms and legs into snowballing, into throwing anything he could find.

Please make it so I don't feel a thing.

They slid round the byre, firing two-handed, Ronald heating, beginning to lose himself, happily angry. "Fucker."

"And you, ya cunt."

Into the yard, panting, Jim unsteadied by his worst word and slowing, clapping at Ronald's shoulder, approving, while Ronald turned, took back his smile, made a stop.

He knew his father's car. Bouncing the last few feet of icy ruts, coming for him, the broad hands clamping the steering wheel, that face. The clap of the door disturbed the crows.

Ronald ran the way he'd be supposed to, fetched his bag, shook off the white of the snow. Back outside and Jim was grinning at his father, which was to be expected: his father was clever and made people like him.

"I'm ready to go now."

Ronald slapped Jim gently on the side of the head and felt sick when he smiled in return—they weren't friends, not the way Jim thought they could be.

It didn't take long to be in the car, under the seatbelt and smelling his father's aftershave and traces of home.

Please make me not feel a thing.

Jim waved as the car pulled away and Ronald waved back, felt the shape of the lie he was making, cold near his face. For a while, the drive was quiet.

Not feel a thing.

"Did you have a good time?" You couldn't tell from his father's voice what he'd done, what he was like.

Ronnie, Ronnie, mad as fuck, mad as fuck, mad as fuck. Ronnie, Ronnie, mad as fuck. Mad. As. Fuck.

"I said, did you have a good time."

"It was all right."

"Just all right."

"Aye." Keeping his face to the window and the dirty brown edge of the road, the tree shapes very thin and scared-looking, "It was all right. Aye."

Further off, the snow was bright, a clean slide of whiteness, turning round them and Ronald here in the middle, so small that he couldn't matter and needn't care. His mother let everything matter, that's why she hurt.

Please not a thing.

But, in time, fear always changed to something different, you just had to wait. He would show her.

It wasn't about wishing, or pretending, and there were no miracles. It was about concentrating until you can turn into somebody new, somebody your father won't expect. Ronald would wait to get older and stronger and then it would happen, he'd make it: he'd be a bad son.

Touch Positive

He was driving to pick up the boxes when he realised what was making him most afraid: the arithmetic. Thirty-five was really hardly anything, not much at all, until you doubled it and then that was seventy, which was a lot, more than someone like him could really bear, he didn't expect to reach as far as that, would be relieved not to. Which meant that he was middle-aged.

Lots of people were middle-aged, most of the people he knew, but they tended to view their condition as being still quite young. They did young things and did not appear ridiculous. Tom wanted to be like them: also still quite young: and sometimes he could, he managed it. But, on his own, he would start to multiply, subtract, and see that he'd run at least half of his way to being dead and the backs of his thighs would tingle and he would see less well, somehow—his distances got blurry—and he would want to break things, but he'd never had the courage to vandalise anything—apart from, possibly, his life—so that would make him more depressed. And the weight of his maths, the chill of it, would also get much worse if he noticed the sun's setting, the big night smothering down, or if there were cut flowers somewhere—dying visibly—or if some idiot on the radio, or at a party, played old records and made him remember the horrible fraying of his time.

A man, perhaps thirty-seven, trotted stupidly into the road and then lost heart, wavered between a staggered retreat and a dash for the centre line. Tom thumped his horn and then watched, moderately pleased, as the man's upper body jerked, his arms flurried, graceless, and he span back to take shelter between the parked cars. Nice to see someone else frightened, someone older.

The parking here was appalling, but that cheered Tom up, too: it wasn't an age-related problem. No one could find a space here, not even a toddler—should a toddler ever try. And judging by the driving he'd seen on his way, the under-fives had already made it, *en masse,* to the open road.

All of which had done nothing for his headache and nor did threading through clotted side streets for twenty minutes until he startled some ragged-haired harridan, worrying her Volvo free of the kerb and two bookending minivans. He resisted every urge to just leap out and scream, and even forced up an encouraging nod when she stalled again. Once she'd finally shuddered off, he tucked himself in with a brief complaint of gears. Reverse hadn't always sounded that alarming, he should take a weekend soon and look at it, do a real overhaul.

For now, though, finding painkillers was his only priority, so he sloped into the chemist and bought his favourite effervescent type. The checkout girl—not a good advertisement for the chain's featured skin-care aids—stared at him when he broke into the package, snapped a tablet in two and then popped half into his mouth. True to form, it swelled bitterly, tickled and started to do its noble work. No more headache, very soon.

"You're not meant to take them like that."

He would, had his mouth not been filling with bile-flavoured, blessedly anaesthetising foam, have answered that he was *especially* meant to take them like that, because that was the way they worked best.

"I mean, you're supposed to have water, if you . . ."

He shrugged at her in the manner of a man thinking *And what on earth would I be doing, wandering about the high street with a glass of water constantly to hand?—I'd have to be mad.* Then he eased the second half of the tablet in through the seal of his lips, winced happily and turned away.

Covering the distance from the chemist to the greengrocer's, he managed to wedge in another two halves, on the move, and could already feel a sunnier disposition taking hold. Once indoors again, things were still a mite unregulated behind his teeth—and his stomach queased once or twice, disrespectfully—so he spent a few minutes pacing, inspecting the organic vegetables—which looked diseased—and the ordinary fruit—which looked toxic. Then, confident of his ability to speak again without frothing, he approached an earth-stained assistant.

"Do you have any boxes, by the way." This *by the way* suggesting that he was primarily a customer and therefore entitled to respect.

"No. Sorry." The man looked a little slow.

"What, none at all?" What the hell did they use, then: sacks, the pockets of their aprons, rustic trugs, did they carry every item in by hand? Tom glowered at the display. "You have oranges."

"I beg your pardon?" He *was* slow, undoubtedly, something about his consonants was stunted.

"You have oranges—over there. Oranges come in *orange boxes.*"

The assistant blinked mournfully across at the incriminating fruit. "We don't keep boxes. We break them up."

"Why?"

"What?" One hand bunched a section of his apron, sluggishly uneasy. Probably he wasn't meant to do things that involved speaking, or meeting customers: probably they tried to keep him shut up in the back, lifting individual potatoes out of vans. His being here at all must be a terrible mistake.

Tom enunciated more clearly, as if he were speaking to someone kept under glass, or under potatoes, someone taking complicated drugs. "WHY DO YOU BREAK THEM UP? WOULD THEY NOT BE MORE USEFUL, NOT BROKEN UP?"

"No." The denial had an animal placidity about it that momentarily urged Tom towards assault.

But he reined in. "I see. Just following orders, then, are you? *Breaking things up.*" Which was the most elegant retort that he could summon at such short notice. He left, frowning, and also projecting an air of apparent sadness; as if, truly shocked by the mindless destruction habitually wreaked on the premises, he was unable to offer them his custom.

The newsagent was just as unhelpful, although more informative. "They pick up the rubbish this morning, so nobody will have much left."

"But I need boxes today. Urgently."

There was a slight, playful shift in the newsagent's expression, he was possibly a man of worldly experience. He may even have been *the* MacLaren, as mentioned in the sign outside: MACLAREN NEWS AND TOBACCONIST. "The supermarket. You could try there. They go through a lot in a day."

"Thank you." Now and then, you did meet people who understood life's difficulties, who were neither pedantic nor soft in the bloody head.

"But they usually send a boy out to compact them."

Again. "Why, for God's sake?"

The possible Mr. MacLaren was edging towards a grin. "Flattened, they take up less space."

"Well, don't we all."

And there he was—*the* MacLaren, it must surely be he—

grinning his head off by this point, taking his time with it, masterly, "Did you want something?" The proprietor in his domain—the way to be, if you could manage it, in control. "I can help you with anything else?" He clearly grinned a lot.

Tom, on the other hand, got very little practice. "Oh, of course." This was an establishment worthy of a purchase. "Yes, a newspaper. A good one."

"Which one do you usually get?"

"I don't." This wasn't wholly true, but suddenly Tom didn't want to pick a paper that might show him in a bad light. "You choose one."

The grin widened, chuckled. "Here then, this'll keep you going." And a fat fold of newsprint was tumped down on the counter. "Good luck."

The paper was not inexpensive, but Tom dumped it in a bin as he headed for the supermarket: it seemed too heavy, in too many parts, and it had an unsettling headline. The colour supplements, he already knew to be wary of: they were either full of young people being effortless, or the elderly being brave, but still plainly past it. They were not things designed for the undeluded and middle-aged reader.

At the supermarket, someone had been baking again, trying to make the place smell homely. Actually the resultant thick, wet fog of desperate vanilla left Tom wanting to gag. He sneezed and halted just before the Tinned Goods aisle could draw him in and realised that he might have come here anyway this afternoon. In a usual weekend, it was quite possible he'd have swung by, gently picked up the better part of a week's stuff for Kate and himself.

He couldn't do that today, because Kate didn't want him to live with her, not any more.

That seemed unlikely. It was hopelessly true, but still not as believable as gathering some shopping and then going home.

But it had been made very clear, or relatively clear, that he couldn't go home.

That was why he needed the boxes. They were going to hold his belongings, because he refused to be moved out in just black, plastic bags: they were demoralising, they implied that everything he owned was rubbish, that he was being thrown away.

Also unlikely, but also the case.

He took a trolley, because it would give him somewhere to lean—it seemed he might want to lean—and he trundled the length of the shelves of canned meats and skirted the counter of fresh. A man in his position, he supposed, should go into a culinary decline, buy baked beans and chocolate biscuits and just-add-hot-water macaroni cheese. To disprove the point, Tom chose some rice for risotto, bagged two handfuls of button mushrooms and then lost interest, simply leaned and walked. It was difficult to shop for food when you didn't have an appetite.

And he might go back and find things had blown over, no more need for individual supplies. This morning hadn't been the time to say that Kate was really over-reacting enormously, but perhaps, in the last few hours, she would have worked that out for herself. He could see that it would have been understandable for her to be upset if he hadn't been going to tell her eventually, but it wasn't as if he had really been keeping a *secret.* He had been keeping *quiet,* that was all. Other men got away with not mentioning criminal actions, previous genders, other families: they told outright lies: Tom had only been waiting for his moment to let her know the truth.

He had lost his job.

It had been upsetting for him, too, traumatic: which she seemed quite unwilling to admit. Tom had worked out a month's notice and been unemployed for a week: trying to get used to it, fighting every kind of personal doubt and alarm. He'd been preparing himself to confess, once he was calmer. Kate couldn't see past the fact that he hadn't told her five weeks ago. This was unreasonable and selfish, which wasn't like her.

Tom had drifted into the Tea aisle and slowed. For some reason, he couldn't remember the type of tea they liked. Kate took it out of the packet and put it into an old tin, a tin that she would have now and he would not. It was a sad drink, anyway, something for the elderly, for a single man borrowing a friend's flat and going off to sit there alone, thinking about having no job, no one to talk to, no way to slow the clock.

And Tony's flat was horrendous, there was no denying that. It was a bottom-of-the-barrel sort of choice: a hormone-coated leftover from the days when Tone was single, when they were all single. Tone talked about renting it out, from time to time, and then would make none of the pressing improvements that might make any well-balanced tenant want to stay. Besides, unoccupied, it was more convenient, because then Tony and his friends could use it. A few of them would stay there every time they had a late night. Tom, Tone, Matt, whoever: they'd spread out on the sofa, the floor—Tone would get the bed—and they'd sleep it off. This was the considerate, gentlemanly thing to do. Cabbies and wives and mothers and girlfriends, they didn't want you trying to get home: being clumsy, noisy, unwell. The best thing for everyone's sake was to head for the flat, crumple, and then start again presentably in the morning. So the place was an asset, undeniably, but it had also suffered a number of terrible insults over the years.

He threw some teabags into the trolley: the round kind. Kate would never have bought them, so they wouldn't make him melancholy. Cleaning things, he'd need them, too: the surfaces were going to be grisly, and the bathroom would be worse.

This was all such a mistake. But Kate wouldn't let him go

through with it, she wasn't cruel. The day would end better than it had started. There was no way it could not. She did love him. She'd mentioned that.

"Excuse me. Do you have any boxes?" His voice sounded gloomy: he'd need to watch, keep his spirits well ordered, no matter what.

The girl rearranging the scouring powders looked round at him, puzzled. "We have tins, or the bottles of cream . . ." She had placid eyes, the eyes of a forgiving woman.

"No. I mean, I need boxes to put things in. Old boxes that you'd be throwing away. I'm moving." He'd tried to make the last sentence neutral, but it shuffled out, laden with suggestions of bereavement, or an otherwise tragic failure of supporting walls.

"Oh." Linda—that was the name on her badge—looked at him with sympathy. "Oh, you would have to talk to Brian at the back." Sympathy would be dangerous now, it could make him turn unstable. "Or I could ask him for you." He didn't fancy bursting into tears, not in a supermarket.

"That would be very kind. Linda."

She flinched at the sound of her name: as if it meant that he'd declared himself her stalker.

"It's on your badge."

Her face had tightened, she swallowed lumpily.

"Your name. On your badge." This was good, she was annoying him now, which gave him a little more energy, less chance of being glum. "How would I contact this Brian?"

Her voice settled, but was still quieter than it had been, and her kind eyes were averted. "At the Customer Service desk." She struggled both arms back into the soapy shelf, avoiding him.

"Thanks. Good of you. Thanks."

As he moved to select the strongest-looking disinfectant, she called after him, "I'll speak to Brian for you first." Because he'd been right, she was the forgiving type.

"Thanks." It would take very little to ease everybody's way in the world: courtesy, gentleness, tiny bits of redemption, perhaps once a month. But there was so much negativity around, these days, and a staggering percentage of it aimed solely at him.

He halted to consider the frozen seafood: one complete freezer was wedged to the brim with identical briquettes of some nondescript grey fish, or fish substitute. You'd never keep cheery, eating that.

And this was when his mind produced, as he'd known it eventually would, the spectre of That Day: his earliest experience of breaking up. Resurrected, yet again, were his grubby overalls, his boots, the patch of mud he stared at while he talked to her, to Melissa, and the sound of her saying, "What do you mean? I don't know what you mean."

He'd been fifteen—young by anyone's reckoning—and working in a stables, not because he liked horses or particularly wanted to ride, but because he'd been anxious to make himself sturdy, imposingly muscular, and couldn't think of any better way. He detested sport. So he'd shifted hay bales and lifted saddles and shovelled manure and piss-soaked straw and had developed nothing more than twine burns and calluses across both hands. He'd kept on, because he was earning money and because—he'd been an idiot not to guess—the stables were almost perpetually haunted by girls: beautifully terrifying women and breathless, well-exercised girls. Occasionally boys would turn up, baggy-jodhpured and hunched, but they were a threat to no one, not even him.

Not that he made his predatory intentions public—he'd liked to be oblique, even back then. Mostly, when the girls were about, Tom would do no more than take the stiffest brush and loudly, manfully, sweep down the cobbles: raising, in the process, a fine mist of shitty water and urine for everyone near to inhale—him first. Or he would lurk in amongst the ponies, solemnly labouring with a curry comb: professional and unapproachable but, each Tuesday, taking his chance to nod curtly at Melissa.

She'd had that soft look, the one that lets bygones be bygones in later life, he'd recognised it instinctively. For months he watched her, learned her: the way she was well turned out, but never prissy, her firm understanding of her mount—Buster, usually—and the shifting, eloquent muscle in her thighs, clearly, harrowingly visible a field away.

He had wanted to kiss her legs. And her mouth. Beyond that, he'd hoped she would understand how to proceed. Thus far, he'd only fumbled round someone at a party, two cans of cider making him bold but imprecise. That hadn't been a success—and he'd felt he was being unfaithful to Melissa, to all he'd have liked to keep for her, lying in wait.

His deepest, most articulate hope had been that perhaps Melissa would let him wank while she was there. That would have made an efficient compromise: something with which he was very familiar, combined with something completely beyond his imagination—and he had tried to imagine it, he really had.

And then, "Do you . . . wouldyoumaybe . . . because I . . ." He had felt his brain dropping away from behind his eyes, failing and starting to rot, "because I really . . ." there was hardly any time, surely, before he'd collapse in a dirty heap like a cast-off set of overalls. "I . . . Melissa."

Of course she hadn't understood him, nobody could. "What do you mean? I don't know what you mean." His emptying head had seemed to lunge up through the thick, sticky air of its own accord and had then discovered it was dreadfully able to watch Melissa's expression move from one of mystification, tinged with fear, towards dawning amusement and then disgust. Everything had stopped once she'd reached disgust.

She hadn't laughed at him, that was a kind of mercy. But

she'd told most of the other girls about him and they had. By the end of the day, he'd been shivering and twitching with angry misery. Mr. Barker, whose steely wife ran the business, had ambled out into the hollow evening with the pay and, for the first time Tom could remember, had become animated.

"No, no. Don't tell me. I can imagine. Little cats, all of them. You come to the house now, come on."

Tom had never been near the house, let alone inside it. Mrs. Barker made it clearly out of bounds. But Mr. Barker's broad, hard arm had landed across his shoulders and gripped, beginning to steer him irresistibly up the bedraggled driveway.

"So, young mister. Know what *you* need, don't you? For troubles of the heart."

Trapped in the brown, dog-smelling living room, Tom shook his head, momentarily troubled by the answers Barker might anticipate. He'd then brightened greatly as Barker had reached down behind the bookcase and lifted up, like a tame rabbit, an almost full bottle of whisky. Mrs. Barker, clearly, was not at home.

They had drunk like men together until it was dark, Barker becoming mildly more relaxed and Tom beautifully intoxicated. It was his introduction to spirits. Before, he'd been afraid of them, but now he discovered that whisky, at least, was a lovable, gentle thing. Barker, a generally thirsty person himself, had been fatherly, limiting Tom's consumption, pacing him and easing him to a place where he was perfectly able to walk the six miles home and yet entirely unable ever to recall the journey. He'd woken in bed, still wearing his socks, but otherwise correctly undressed. And the row he'd got at breakfast was untarnished, miraculously, by any kind of hangover: they were another peril of middle age, recriminations burrowing in through a nauseous headache, they didn't do that when you were a child.

Tom's trolley had silted up with a despondent mound of toiletries and cleaning cloths, frozen prawns, chicken legs and pizzas, a loaf of bread. Half of this would go off, it was too much for one person. One person, currently all he could manage to be.

The fabled Brian—most surprisingly—was waiting at the Customer Service desk when Tom trudged up with his pointlessly straining carrier bags. Linda had kept her promise, so God bless Linda. But there were just five boxes, no more, and all of them flat.

"They'll work fine, though. You have to fold them back up and put a bit of tape . . ."

Tom was nodding bitterly, "Flattened, they take up less space."

Brian seemed about to begin a demonstration of exactly how handy containers for everything on earth that you still have left could be fashioned from such an unpromising stack of cardboard. Tom could feel his bags tugging him down, stooping him, as if years were passing while he stood. "No."

Brian darted a step away from the would-be boxes, said nothing more.

"No. I understand. You're giving me what I deserve, that's fine." What Tom really wanted was another painkiller, but it would be awkward to take one now. In the car—he could hang on until then. "I'll take my bags out to the car and then I'll come back. Or I could take a trolley."

Either because he didn't especially want Tom to come back, or feared that he might abscond in an act of dastardly trolley theft, Brian volunteered to carry the boxes back to Tom's car.

"Are you a drinking man, Brian?"

This was a stupid thing to ask: Brian gave every indication of being twelve and afflicted by some variety of blight: a decent drink would cripple him—more than he already was. "Hm? A drinking man?" Even so, Tom was trying to put the boy at ease, start a spot of casual banter, it didn't remotely matter what they might banter about.

Still, Brian appeared deeply taxed by the simple query—*A drinking man?*—and Tom wondered if he should have said *person, child, midget*—if he should have specified what he meant by *drinking*—if he'd intended the verb should pertain to liquids of any kind, or be restricted to those of the intoxicating type. Perhaps Brian absorbed his moisture in some less straightforward, less oral, way. Tom would not have put it past him.

Then a response gargled out, "No, no, ah, not really. Don't drink. Much."

"Not really? Well, good. It can cause many, many problems." Drinking actually did no such thing—but this was probably the proper line to take with someone like Brian: a wheezy, imbecilic dwarf. Christ, what would *that* be like if it ever got pissed?

"Here we are then—my car." The dent in the passenger door was more than usually obvious in this light. Brian appeared to be hypnotised by its severity. "Splendid, then, young Brian." Tom beamed, rather paternally, he thought, but Brian now regarded him as if he were, at least, a convicted hit-and-runner. "You have been so helpful. May I give you a tip." Brian retreated as though the pound coin Tom extended was, in some way, venomous. "Ah, well, then. Cheers."

Predictably enough, though, a doughy, clammy hand did dart in and snatch the pound just before Tom could pocket it again. Some people had no principles. Brian retreated without a backward glance. He walked, when you studied him, as if he had one leg shorter than the other, or one foot thinner than the other, Tom wasn't sure how you would tell.

Tom unlocked the boot and then halted, gridlocked by a choice of packing strategies. He could put the flattened boxes in first and the carrier bags on top, which probably made more geometrical sense and implied that he would arrive home, unpack the shopping, engage in a tricky but not insoluble conversation with Kate and then never have to come out and fetch the boxes, let them moulder. Or he could put the shopping in first and then the boxes, which was the less stable solution and suggested that he would arrive, pack up his things, perhaps in a savagely empty house, and then leave for Tony's flat, driving towards the type of sharp, unfamiliar horizon that would put any man of intelligence in mind of an oncoming blade.

He hoisted up the carriers—why call them that? What kind of bags *didn't* carry? It was a wholly unnecessary adverb—no, adjective, something like that. And then his thinking clogged, jolted, and his arms began to shake and he was sobbing, weeping, blind with it.

Wouldn't do, wouldn't do at all. A man crying into his car. No one to care about it. That was too sad.

He remembered Mr. Barker taking his glass that one evening to refill it. His hand had briefly ringed Tom's wrist, and, full to his face and whisky-breathed, he'd crooned, "You know us? People like us? We're like the horses. Yes, we are. We're touch positive. You press against us, even hit us, and we lean in to feel more. We like touching. We're not ourselves without it." Tom hadn't quite understood what Barker meant, but he'd learned since. And it was true, he was touch positive. He was not himself without it.

He snatched up the boxes, threw them in, everything smeared and stinging when he blinked, shut the boot and brailed his way to the car door, slid into the driver's seat.

Glove compartment.

No.

Under the passenger seat, then.

No.

Shit. He couldn't have lost it. It couldn't have walked away.

Inside that stupid pannier thing in his door—that was it, that was it.

Yes. Mercy, yes.

A half-full quarter bottle of Gordon's. That was to say, an eighth bottle.

Silly.

Silly thing to think.

Unscrewing the cap, Tom already felt softly calmer and then, after a moderate sip, that first little race, he began to inhale and exhale like a human being. If he'd thought of this sooner, the day would have fitted him better. Never mind, though, this was all right.

He felt, felt, well, he felt at home—his genuine home, if not fully arrived, then on the way. But gin could make you depressed if you didn't take measures, so he sucked in another half-painkiller—keep things perky—caffeine and codeine—grand.

Tom hadn't noticed before this, but right down the length of the street there were chestnut trees: those heavy, lobed leaves shifting, calm and so full of green, roaring with it. There were birds, too, somewhere, letting out small, good-natured songs that no one could have heard without being lifted. This really was an ideal day; he had been hurrying too much to notice. Lucky that he'd taken time out, adjusted his attitude, that was the sort of thing to keep you young in many of the ways that really mattered.

He stole another minor tot from the bottle before stowing it again, dried his face and started the engine: it caught at once, full of pep. This was a good sign and implied—absolutely *did* imply, because all things in the universe were connected—that it was possible, realistically possible, that he'd go and see Kate next, determined and perfectly able to talk her round. It did strongly suggest that. He would apologise, of course, and, because she loved him—had said so—he would persuade her that their relationship could be altered in useful and constructive ways and—this was the main point—persevered with and *saved*. Why give up now?

God, it was a lovely afternoon.

Shame to waste it.

What he ought to do was go into the Captain's Rest: Tony might be there by this time, or someone, or it didn't matter, Tom could be sociable with absolutely anyone, he was easygoing, always had been—especially friendly to one and all. He could dash in there, just have a whisky, gather his thoughts, prepare and be on his way. He could drink one for old Barker: for horse-hearted men. Of course, God bless them.

And, after that, he would go home to his girlfriend—Kate was still his girlfriend, these things didn't change, not fundamentally—and he'd tell her that he was sorry and that they would be OK and she would believe him, because he was nothing but truth this afternoon, it was aching all through him like a lovely bruise.

By the end of this afternoon—the start of this evening—that was better yet—once he was composed and warmed thoroughly—such processes took time—he would go and see her. Absolutely. There would be a moment today and he would reach it and he would catch it and understand that he would be ready to see her then, he would be ready perfectly.

Indelible Acts

It wasn't difficult.

"That's nice. Very nice."

Anyone could have done it—absolutely anyone.

"Just the way I like you. Great."

He'd been applying the usual friction, first and second fingertips. "Mm. Now the right," the circular rub and flicker, insisting against cloth, until both nipples caught at his attention, perked and ached. The way they would.

"Good." His lips slackened, moist, while his interest hid in the dumb black of his glasses. "Very good." Laurie paused next, smiling, satisfied, happy my needs were symmetrically prominent. "Nice."

But anybody with hands could have done as much. Not even *hands*, necessarily: *hand* would have been enough; or a half-way decent prosthetic: even a properly placed domestic pet. Laurie wasn't working miracles—he was not involved with raising up the dead—only a little prickle or two of extremely erectile flesh. Brush or fluster them, breathe at them, kiss, and they'll button up tight, they'll crest. Within their particular limits, the more you choose to find them, then the more there'll be to find— that's how they work, their inclinations are naturally salient. I can't do a thing to change them and neither can he—not funda-mentally. A simple chill can prick them, as can that certain monthly tenderness, and then I'll be edged near precisely the same old slip of wet intentions he rubbed me to.

Traffic coughed and worried in the road beside us, pedestri-ans passed, among them a higher than average number of priests—or just men in cassocks, I'm not an expert, I can't say—and I wanted, very simply, to pummel Laurie on to his back and in some way secure him, then cut him out naked at the waist and suck him until both his balls were small as raisins, until he cried.

Because such impulses are irresistibly instinctive, they can't be helped. Primed past the point of caring, by no matter what or whom, I will react entirely predictably. Like the leopard with the zebra, like the lobster with the pot, I am part of nature's usual arithmetic. I do often try to remember this in order to build per-spective, an independently distant view.

Four nuns pattered by, soundless, their faces a little unlikely, surprised to be marooned in wimples. My breath barked against my sternum, abrasively needy, while social convention and men-tal discipline struggled to keep me from arrest. I said nothing, did nothing, only seethed, as might have been expected, queasy with lust.

Laurie grinned, knowingly unscathed. "You like it just as much as I do, don't you. Hm?"

"But not now." The day basted the avenue pleasantly: foreign monuments roiling under a classical sun and the Colosseum dark at Laurie's shoulder, a monstrous hoop of decay.

"Why not now?"

"Because people are looking, people will see."

"Then you shouldn't have worn that blouse—that's why they're looking, so of course they'll see. Don't you like men star-ing at your tits? I do. Because they can't have you. Because you're mine."

Because you're mine. It's a standard wording, fits any mouth. I would have liked to turn it back on him, set *my* voice kicking in *his* chest, arcing that customary charge of hopefulness between the stomach and the throat. I would have liked to make it clear that

Because you're mine I will stand in the midst of clergy, stiff with the thought of your foreskin, bitten back. Because you're mine I will be—with insufficient warning—simultaneously furious, beguiled, delighted, affronted, murderous and cheap. Because you're mine I will watch you the way that I'm watching right now and remember that I can strip you full down to the pink, the quick. I know you at least as well as you know me.

Because you're mine. It's a standard wording, not dependent upon truth.

He's pacing now, almost trotting, round the walls, being interested about foundations and seating arrangements and herringbone brickwork, as displayed in flights of steps. He has an enthusiasm for constructions that I find I cannot share. But this is not a problem—I can sit here and write my letter while he prods about. And I can look at him moving through shudders of heat, the firmness of his shadow stretching, snug beneath him. He should wear a hat, really; by this evening he'll have burned. Laurie can be very cavalier about that kind of exposure.

I tend to be more careful, because I have good skin. Most women of my age and younger have fine lines and visible wrinkles, but I don't. I have elasticity and bloom. I catch myself sometimes in the mirror when I'm alone and there it is—my beautiful outside—the ghosts of his hands still across it from the afternoons and evenings he's spent examining, testing flexibilities. I give him my best and he does appreciate it, he does take the time to say.

I also give him my collaboration, my consent, my long Bank

Holiday weekend to pack up and use in a curtained and mirrored hotel room, in the moist, ecclesiastical heat of Rome. Since we flew in last night we've transgressed without dispensation, hourly, perhaps because no one who matters is here to see. I could, for example, cross to him now, take his hand, stroke the blue push of veins at his wrist and wriggle our palms together in an unmistakably familiar, casual, mutually affectionate and incriminating way that any malign observer could use against us. But this is a safe city, we have left Greenwich Mean Time and entered anonymity.

This makes Laurie happy, I can tell. His shoulders have a buoyancy about them I only normally see at night. In the dark he unfolds, relaxes, takes me outside, moves me up and down pavements we can't share with any kind of comfort in open day. Or else, he goes out driving, and I choose to come along, be where he takes me.

"Here?"

"Why not?" That time, we were in a field—lots of fresh air, healthy. "It's quiet, there's no one around." But his eyes still flickered across the windows, checking. Although he enjoys observing, Laurie never wants to be observed. He has a fear of being cornered, or forced into actions he won't wish to take. "No interruptions, hm?"

I noted the bluey green of sheep's eyes, reflecting far off to the right. "It's raining."

"So you'll get wet."

He put on the handbrake and he turned the engine off and we sat in his car in the overcast dark of the field. No stars. On other nights, he might have picked the forest, or the underground office car park. I removed my mackintosh, kept on my shoes. High heels—impractical over the stubble of wheat.

"Oh, yes. Just what the doctor ordered. Let me see, though. Let me really see."

Because I wished to do so, needed to do so, had waited to do so, because this is a choice that I can make, I stepped out and crossed the shorn rows to show him my skin. The bright burn of me flared in the headlamps, gleaming with drizzle and then moving, extinguishing under him.

"You're a very naughty, dirty girl."

Held safe between him and his car, I could feel his gloves against my spine, the thin chill of a zip, the tongue and groove of our mutual interest, of us being us together, our recoiling fit. I'd turned my head and could watch the blisters of rain on the bonnet shiver and split: a dim shining, level with my eye.

He could have been anybody, "Lift your arse," but he was Laurie, working me tight with a smooth negation of all other possibilities.

I was glad of him, his cover, his cloth heat. My mother had often warned me against night air and stormy weather and being caught without a coat. Which made another reason to let Laurie catch me and—in a sense—lend me his.

"Good girl."

Anticipation faded into the sink of earth, the vague scent of animal shit and wet wool. He pressed my breath into fits and starts and came, as always, silently in a ragged burst of motion and then stillness, withdrawal. He's taught himself to be thoroughly secretive.

Which is why I've learned to read his body and his things. This afternoon I can tell he is contented, easy: he doesn't push at his hair too much, or tug his ears, and there is something liquid in his stride, a muscular amusement, a tiny swing of appetite.

He's dressed to be comfy, but not unattractive. I saw him, warm and freshly woken, maybe seven hours ago, picking the right things and strolling between the wardrobe and the bed, naked in a way that made my gums hurt, made the palms of my hands start to twitch. I am designed to experience these feelings, they are hard-wired through my whole anatomy. I consider types of insulation, circuit breaking, but every time, he trips the switch and seems to prove I couldn't end this, that anything else would be inadequate.

Today, for example, he has equipped himself to show that he is happy and to jump-start my skull: white boxers (the pair I bought him) and his oldest jeans, because we both know they hang well and make it look more than likely that he does, too. Add in the plain black T-shirt to set off the linen jacket for thumb-hooking over his shoulder and the Ray-Bans for making sure that he won't need to squint and there he is, my Laurie, all tooled up.

Back at home, he'll leave clothes with me: accessories, bits and bobs: small records of his scent and shape. Leather is most eloquent; his belts roll where they've taken the curve of his back and notch to mark the measure of his waist, his shoes and gloves reform against his movements and his sweat. And, of course, I do the same. In his absence, the pattern of his previous needs sings out on me. He's oiled into the grain of my fingers the way any habit would be. It is unsurprising that, at night, I can find his memory shunts me into sleeplessness.

I haven't tried to sleep in Rome, not yet. It has seemed unnecessary. Fatigue occasionally dives at me, unsteadies reality, but I won't give in. I'm going to stay more than conscious, because Laurie is all here with me: leant over the railing, nicely taut and shifting: my encyclopaedia. Before we leave, before it's over, I'll know his arms by heart, from the short clip of his fingernails to the paler and paler tenderness of his joints, the soft rise of hair. Anyone can concentrate, stay alert, for only four days and three nights when they're constantly accompanied by the body they've learned to miss. I am always greedy for what I know I'll lack.

Of course, this rationing and waiting will tend to breed intensity in us both.

"Tell me where to aim it."

The accumulated discomfort of over-rehearsed desire.

"Or I'll just put it where I want."

In Rome, I'm moving from the bite of his imagination to his everyday coughs and whispers, his small breaths when he's reading and the way he towels his hair. Each part of this is as addictive as I'd guessed, as hard to walk away from, or to fight.

"I'll put it where I want it. And you know where I'll want . . ."

I'm more used to the short nights when we're trying to impress. They were when I pushed for something to stay with me while he did not, for marks, for brands in the memory, indelible acts. I have, in the past, been anxious to experiment with error and trial: squatting, or standing, or bending, or lying in my bath.

"*That's* where I'll want. Right there. And there."

"Laurie . . ." The not unpleasant smell of it, slightly bitter, grassy, hot. "Laurie, could you—"

"What?"

"Well. It isn't . . . erotic."

He was standing unfastened, braced. "I'm *pissing on you,* how can that not be erotic?" He rubbed through his fringe with his free hand.

"It's mainly just warm—more relaxing than anything. I'm sorry."

"It's not erotic." His flow relented, sputtered, stopped. "Not at all?"

"I'm sorry."

He sat on the edge of the bath with his back to me, set his hands on his knees to lean forward and away. "No, don't be sorry."

"It was good to try."

"Yeah." He looked at his watch. "I don't really have time now for anything else."

I hate Laurie's watch. Resistant to many varieties of highly unnatural shock and proofed against pressures and waters at hideous depths, it will most certainly outlive us. It pecks through our time together, unrelenting, it's his conscience and my limit and I wish he'd agreed to just leave it in our room. I don't want to be reminded of when we'll stop. I don't want to be sad yet and have to tell him why.

I want to keep collecting and making his inventory complete without distractions. When I go home, he'll have soaked my recollection, my blood will smell of him, I will think with his voice and be able to be alone, to be with *other* people, and to comfortably keep in mind all I'll need of him.

I do hope that, eventually, this could be true: that Laurie could come to be anyone, the next one, someone new.

He's craning over. He shouldn't do that, it leaves the skin between his hair and his collar bared to the sun. He's tender there, sweet to kiss, and this is not what he *does*: something repeatable, replaceable, easy to find again. This is what he *is*. This is the unrepeatable, irreplaceable, unforgivable man I have had to do without for years, holding on, numb between instalments of whatever his household arrangements allow him to give. This is the best he can bring me: it's what should have stopped us becoming ridiculous.

This should have prevented the evenings full of ice cubes and safety razors and fruit and all the other variations on our theme—a little sting of toothpaste, a little KY dip, escalating restraint.

"Dirty girl."

"No, you're the one that's dirty. Dirty old man."

He only grinned, untying me, showing he'd taken no offence. "No, *you're* the one and you're going to prove it. Go and get that thing—I want to see. Show me how you're a bad girl— playing while I'm away . . ."

"The people at work bought it for me."

"But you use it."

"Yes, I do."

I fetched it through for him, still in the box, so that he could unveil it.

"Fuck."

My implement was longer, fatter—unmistakably larger than his.

Which should have been of no significance to him. At least a couple of inches were just there for grip, they weren't a requirement, they didn't establish a level of need.

He turned it in his hands like a condensed adultery.

"Fuck."

But I don't think he ever considered not using it.

"All right, then. All right." The dark of his eye cold, mirroring my skin. "You always want things to remember . . . Well, all right."

And I do remember, absolutely clearly, the moment when the pain of his being there exceeded the pain of his having to leave me be.

Laurie and I, we don't discuss that night: it's our other secret. We don't tell.

But I find, more and more, that I write out what happened, what happens, in letters I never post—letters to a wife I do not know. Although we must have a few things in common, that's what I'd suppose. We must both look at him, walking in sunlight, and find him beautiful.

Elsewhere

This is where you end up, then, your last resort.

It was the town's eighty-seventh annual rodeo—which meant they'd been doing this in James Bridge for eighty-seven years. Somehow, that made it worse.

"Big day for the Alberts. Biggest day of the year." Francis Albert nudged her. "And front-row seats." Grinning down at his programme: "She's going to be a winner. Oh, yah." He spoke calmly, softly, Francis Albert, always took his time, no matter what.

This is where you end up. Sitting on a temporary rake of wooden benches under this long, flat afternoon, the edge of the seat behind her beginning to nag her hip. *From Stirling, to Glasgow, to Sligo and then the big one—Montreal. And after that, you're here, nowhere but here.*

The wind was busy, pawing at the dust. A new, snapping breeze veered to worry the heat from the sunlight and pick up another thin jolt of 70s rock—courtesy of the 70s speaker system—and shake it until its sense fragmented.

Out in the ring, one of the many Alberts yelled to herself as she turned her horse, tight between barrels, threaded an imagined clover leaf over the sand, and then leaned up and forward into a sprint, one arm wide. Francis Albert also lifted his voice: deliberate, supportive: "*Carla. Yes. That girl,*" his manner so placid that he might have been murmuring, telling a stranger the best way to Round Lake.

As it turned out, Carla's time wasn't the fastest, wasn't even that close. "Well, who would believe it." Francis Albert folded his programme—six sheets of photocopied typing and blurred ads—and pinched it into a cheerfully reproachful crease.

"Sorry."

"That's the luck I have, eh." He was nodding to someone she couldn't see, "You understand the luck I have?" chuckling at a point beyond her head, his sentences entirely tranquil, a clear, unruffled atmosphere about him, nothing that could ever have been touched by a misfortune. "Every time, a new disaster: you know?" He was enjoying this now, playing on the lie of his awful life—making it so plainly untrue that it couldn't count as a deception. "Eh, Juney?" He wanted her to play, as well.

But June didn't. "I'm not sure." She kept her expression quiet, close to neutral.

"It doesn't change . . ." He eased this out to her, making one last try, as she stood up, coughed.

"No." She studied the thin film of grey that had gathered on her hands; pause for any length of time in this wind and you silted up: you never just got air here, nothing so simple. "No, I suppose not." She coughed again and tasted broken stone and a trace of the dirt of animals.

"You headed off?"

"I think so."

When she started to walk, she hunched down slightly, a concession to those whose view she must be spoiling, and Francis Albert said, "I'll see you around, then," in the same gentle way she'd heard him talk about her that Friday—*I can't see anyone rid-*

*ing **her**, bare belly.* The two men he was with, their backs to her:
everyone's backs to her: had both given a small, damp laugh—
*That Juney Morris? I can't see anyone riding **her**, bare belly*—and
then they'd discussed other women while she'd turned away and
rounded the corner again, retraced the route to her house and sat
inside it, breathless.

Still, Francis Albert had meant her no harm. He'd just been
making what was, for him, a factual statement when he couldn't
have known she was near. It wasn't his fault if she made such an
ugly fact, or if she felt angry and clumsy and naked whenever
they met.

And last year it hadn't been true, not in the spring of last
year. Four hours back along the road in another stupid, tiny
town: driving in beside the man who'd brought her, who wanted
to show her the family house, open it up for her—make them a
new beginning in an old place.

She'd stepped from the car with his feel still on her, the
shape of him from when they'd pulled over because he had to
fuck—the way he'd had to in the motel before that—had to. The
heat in her had made the main street blink, turned her walk
smooth and even. She'd helped him to feel young—he told her.

Now sometimes she'd wake with the choke of his tongue in
her mouth, his head in her hands with a tenderness they'd never
really shared. It wasn't a memory, more a joke. An old man getting heavy, getting scared by the difference between their skins.

He went back to his wife. June didn't get the chance to tell
him that he'd been a compromise: her try at settling for comfort,
for less than second best.

Stirling, Glasgow, Sligo. Always west. West as far as James Bridge.

Any further and she'd be in the Pacific, Russia, China: be
washed right back to where she'd started, still a bad fit for her
home.

The space that she'd left on the bench was narrowing as

people shifted and relaxed and the seam between whites and natives closed. It was nothing official, only the usual border that fixed itself whenever the town and the reservation met. Nobody was impolite about it: the groups would simply always separate: apparently friendly, but clearly defined. And, without intending, she would inevitably drift out to a margin, a place where the two incompatibles brushed in the crowd. After ten months in James Bridge, she wasn't sure if she arranged this herself, subconsciously, or if both communities edged her into it, knowing she wasn't a part of either one.

A child watched her from the slope near the corrals, toddler-plump shins and bare feet planted beneath the hem of an adult T-shirt, everything ghosted over with the unavoidable ash brown. His only other colours were the blue in his eyes and the blackish line of wet dirt round his lips that showed where he'd licked them. She tried smiling, but he looked away.

And then the dry tamp of boot heels closed to her left and brought, "Hey, Juney, you having a good time?" The question put with just enough incredulity to rankle.

"Yes. I am enjoying myself. Thank you." Her answer also lively with the sense that this was remarkably unlikely. "And how about you, Freddie?"

Not that she couldn't guess. Of course he was having a good time—if not a great one—she should never doubt it: he was Freddie Williamson, son of Freddie Williamson, who was himself son of another in a line of Christ knew how many other desperately unimaginative Freddie bloody Williamsons. The whole clan of them probably spent their winter nights together, reading the list of their forebears aloud from the family bible like one continuous, sad, baptismal stammer. The rodeo's annual horse sports and beery sideshows must represent a frenzy of fun for any self-respecting member of the clan.

Freddie nodded, sharp, letting her sense his attention against her: the way he was reading her clothes, her hair, every sign that set her outside this life and made her at fault. "That's the roping started . . ." He winked, gave a brief twitch of his head towards the arena where a light-haired man was kneeling and bundling up the feet of a calf with rope, as if he were tying a small cow bouquet. Another man, also light-haired, watched from horseback while the drilling voice of the MC monotoned through a narration.

"And a pretty good time, there, for the MacDonald brothers."

The calf, left duly secured with the proper knot, rocked and jerked, bawling into the sand, failing to work free.

"Come on now, let's give them a big hand."

Somebody whooped from high on the benches and there was a break or two of applause. Freddie swung back to her, serious, testing her defences, "They lost a few points when they caught her . . ." She waited for some kind of punch line. "But you'll have noticed that, Juney, I'm sure: being aware of the way that we keep score." His stare held until she met it, accepted his pointed absence of respect, the dig of something else, a hotter complication in his thought.

"Actually, Freddie, I'd prefer it if you called me June. My name is June." But most names changed here: Freddie, Juney, Marcy, Fancy: like a roll call of Snow White's less successful dwarfs. Which could have been charming but wasn't, even though she had to live amongst them, ought to be glad when they made her sound like a proper neighbour for Jimmy and Billy and Sandie and Lizzie May.

Freddie pressed in another glance, let it search her for too long. "Well, better get back to my wife," and then fired off the parting smile—*I am a working man which is the best type of man there is and I work hard and deserve all that I've got and what I've got is everything you lack: the right to be here and to be at ease here and the right to fuck.*

The dumpy brunette who waited for him over by the hot-dog stall wasn't really his wife, he only called her that, but they lived together on Williamson land and went to church as a couple and bred Williamson children with blunt regularity—June had seen a teenage pair of them scuffling by the calf pens earlier. Sometimes Freddie went back to driving a truck for extra cash and never said how he spent his nights away, but liked to give the impression they were usually wakeful and in active company. It was hard to tell which he enjoyed more: his public almost-adultery, or his almost-wife's humiliation.

This had been the first town fact that June had learned: Freddie Williamson wants it known he screws around. Also several other husbands and wives were not legally husband and wife and the Waldrons' first son had drowned and they wanted another and Mrs. Timms would shoplift, then return what she took by post and Wally Andrews was a torment to his wife, but when he was half drunk she'd feed him dog's meat and when he was all drunk and passed out she'd kick him until he bled: everyone knew everything by heart. The town maintained a dangerous silence by holding itself to ransom repeatedly.

But there have to be occasional mistakes.

*That Juney Morris—I can't see anyone riding **her** bare belly.*

That Juney Morris.

Anyone she met today would have heard it by now and would hear it again when they thought of her, spoke to her, saw her in the street. It would be her set accompaniment, the permanent whisper of who she really was.

Except that I'm not called Juney. And they have no idea of me.

Which hadn't stopped them from winding her down into their stories, because this was what they did. They mashed realities in together and then span them out again, altered, to pass the time. There was altogether too much time here, so a person's eccentricities and sins were trotted out for entertainment, along with their favourite hymn, say, or a soft spot for canned peaches, an ability to mend refrigerators, the odd things they had dreamed of during childhood fevers. She was more secretive than they liked, so they made up gossip to fill out some of her many deficiencies.

They wanted a reason for why she was alone. So they said she'd had some accident, some illness, or she'd lost her first love, or lost one that was true. She wished they were right, but knew that she had no excuses.

"We say the weather does it."

"What?"

That was Mrs. Parsons, Marjory Parsons—please, why don't you call her Margie?—June's employer, but she'd rather be her friend.

"The weather."

Margie had been trying to explain things again, using the slightly over-articulated voice she reserved for ugly children and the elderly and June. No one had set foot inside the shop for that whole morning—it wasn't a day when the train came, so there were no tourists and Mrs. Timms didn't wander by until after lunch. So Margie, huge and oddly soft, as if she'd been filleted, had relaxed into her favourite, didactic mode, letting her eyes half close and folding her sagging arms—something which always made June nervous, in case this time there would finally be more elbows than were normal, more bends than a person with bones could painlessly sustain.

A pause had sunk into place, one that Margie had apparently intended to be expectant.

Well, not that I want to ask you and not that I want you to answer, or need any more of that fine, old James Bridge wisdom, but there is so much time here in every day and we do have to pass it— like kidney stones, or piss . . .

June cleared her throat, "The weather?"

"The wind—you must have noticed, dear."

I am not your dear, nor anyone else's.

Margie had blinked her glossy, bovine eyes. "It only ever stops in the summer, when you need it to clear the bugs. And, of course, all the rest of the time, it picks up every word and stirs what we tell each other around and sets it down where it doesn't belong exactly. But it gets a good home." She smiled.

So it hasn't a thing to do with your own and everyone else's pathological need to intrude. Well, glad to hear it: really happy we've got that clear.

Clicking her tongue, Margie had reached into the breast pocket of her work shirt and had retrieved a dusty cellophane morsel that June knew would turn out to be a fruit candy of some kind, warmed to the temperature of flesh.

"No, that's OK."

"Come on, now." It was advanced, balanced on a palm with roughly the dimensions of an overstuffed paperback. "A face that sour needs a little sweetness." Nothing unkind about this, only a touch of domestic urgency, as if Margie were asking her to mop up a kitchen spill, or go out and stop the dog from barking. There could be no rogue expressions in Margie's shop: not sad, not ironic, not irritated past enduring: only smiles, good, genuine smiles, were tolerated. And the strange thing was that June often produced them. Margie's maternal tone should have grated, *did* grate in a distant way, but it also seemed to soak June with a pleasant paralysis. When Margie told her what to do, she felt comfortably childlike, lighter, susceptible to the hope that all harms could truly be defeated by the unflinching application of homilies and clichés and simple-minded gestures.

That day, she'd taken the sweet. She always did.

. . .

June watched the sponsored tractor lurch out and flatten the arena surface, raking back and forth through rolls of self-inflicted dust. The MC informed everybody who cared that the bull-riding would start up very soon. Riders in lurid shirts, weirdly pristine hats and protective body braces were already bunched along the fence to the rear of the chutes. There was, as Margie might say, no end to the strange things that people would do to get happy.

June, for example, took Margie's sweets, because they made her happy and sentimental and because June knew that she'd indulged in very simple-minded gestures of her own.

One gesture, anyway: she set fire to things. Just before she left a place, she would gather up all of the clothes she had been too alone in, or ones that the wrong hands had touched: letters, pictures, diaries, unfortunate ornaments: everything that could remind her of whatever had gone wrong. Something always had gone wrong. And then she would sprinkle the whole collection with lighter fluid or meths and burn her sadnesses away. It saved having to pack.

Landlords would find her gone and their gardens smoky, lawns scorched, once a back window cracked with heat.

When she first met Margie, June had been leaving James Bridge and making her customary preparation. Handfuls of papers had gone on first with a little clean wood—she'd learned that her pyres weren't self-sustaining, tending to produce a cool, messy blaze, likely to be choked by its own debris. This time she was lucky, a kitchen chair she'd always found depressing had broken up nicely and was providing the heart of her fuel. She fed on a synthetic blouse and watched it wither to a dark, solid mass.

"Clearing out?" Margie had crept round the house and across the lawn without June noticing. Margie was uncannily quiet for someone so large.

"Yes. Soon." Then June had realised that the question hadn't intended to ask if she was leaving, only if she was destroying things for which she had no further need. "I mean, yes." Her eyes must have been noticeably wet, they'd felt wet, but this could have been excused by the smoke which had already lifted in a long, black flag for the length of the block, dirty feathers of paper ash rising inside it unevenly. "Too much smoke. Sorry." She had squinted slightly by way of an additional admission.

But Margie had stood, had studied her slowly, as if she were eyeing a horse, judging the possible bloodline of June's unhappiness. Then Margie reached out with the first of many sweets, "For when bitter things happen—we do all have to swallow them, but we can at least sugar them up."

The moment was ridiculous: June slurring through it, keeping her mind on the fire, aware of the breeze tilting, wheeling to press against her face, and of this stranger with her nonsense and her sweet: a more than plump middle-aged woman in jeans and a flannel shirt. The town was full of them: women who wore tennis shoes and practical, mannish haircuts, who seemed to be lost behind layers of disuse.

June kept her hair long. The dirt and the winds and the alkali water had turned it brittle and she couldn't comb it any more, could only use a brush to fight the snags and tangles: a full half-hour to yank it into order, tug until her head ached and she was ringed with a litter of broken strands. She wouldn't give it up, though.

It's mine, it's years of me, I made it. You have to keep something with you when you go.

She had felt it ragging out behind her, unwieldy.

Margie had coaxed. "Come on now. I got plenty more." Margie had smiled. "My name is Margie." Margie had smiled again, this time making it bigger.

Difficult to hate her, even though June had wanted to. Margie was so plainly a good person, doing a good thing, which nevertheless forced June to drop the stick she'd been using to tend the flames and made her hold her own body tight around the return of a sick pain and then start to cry fully, letting it stifle in. She was too tired to move on again, but she didn't want to stay.

No one sees my hair the way they should do any more. They don't touch it, now they maybe never will. They won't breathe against it. They won't find me out.

A gust had shoved past her while the threat of the rest of her life had rattled, spat, drew blood in all the customary places.

Then she'd rubbed her face with the back of one hand and used the other to take Margie's gift, blinking and sniffling, baffled momentarily by the wrapper, and then closing her mouth around the sweet. It was cherry.

"God works in us."

Their meeting, for Margie, had been just another example of intervention from on high. She had thought she was leaving her house to go and complain about the smoke from a neighbour's fire and, what did you know, instead, she had been presented with a newcomer in despair. It had been her duty to help, or to help God help. In her opinion, there was no difference between the two.

According to Margie, the whole of the rodeo would be seething with God's helpful works. Patty Block, strolling with an emptied beer bottle, perhaps meaning to throw it away, was actually taut with God's intentions, steered towards that nod to Mr. Parker and then delivered into that chat with Bobby Lomax for reasons which were God's alone. Margie's God was a tireless handyman, constantly tinkering. You couldn't tell where or when He might dip in.

But Mr. Parker gets a nod because he almost ran over Patty's daughter, not paying attention while he reversed, and then blamed the girl for being careless. Mr. Parker and Patty don't speak, there's nothing between them but uncivil nods. And Bob Lomax flirts with Patty because he feels sorry for her, although neither of them will take it any further and that won't be the only bottle that Patty empties this afternoon.

The James Bridge air was doubly unsettled, wicked with sand and the twist of invisible insults inflicted and received, the raw balance of hypocrisies, the jar and slide of halted, permitted, invited, avoided and frustrated sex. A fraction of the grit in your teeth would always be bitter with sex.

And I do want to be wrong about this. I would love God to be here with His every intervention plain. It wouldn't have to be for me—I'd welcome assistance for anyone, just so that I could see. But there's nothing to see, there isn't any sign from Him, because He is either absent or elsewhere.

Margie told her to pray—"God likes to hear strange voices"— and Margie certainly repeatedly prayed herself for healing and guidance and lost valuables and natural disasters and the aid of foreign women with a history of starting fires. "You don't want to work in the bar—that's what's getting you down. And, listen, I need someone helping me out in the shop—and that ought to be you—to pick up the crafts from the reservation—you can drive, can't you?"

So, every Wednesday morning, I do get to leave here and then, every Wednesday evening, I come right back. I never pass through the reservation and go on. I fetch what I'm meant to, deliver it safely, exactly as Margie expects. I pack dream-catchers up in cellophane to keep them from the dust. I price calumets and beadwork, arrowheads. I watch Mrs. Timms steal the same silver bracelet, week after week. I buy hand-made herbal conditioner and night cream and soap and my hair is still hard and my hands still crack and my face still tightens, I still blacken the flannel each time I wash. I am dried-out and dirtied all the time.

The chute gate shuddered open to an incongruous slide of disco guitars and a bull span out, lunging, the man on its back jerking inexorably down to the left, and a last, wide, hopeless swing of his free arm, then a scrambling fall, an escape run to the fence. The bull cantered to a ploughing stop, flicked its head, the muscle pumping and twitching in its neck, unpleasantly equal to the weight of so much skull.

I'm starting to understand the other women, why they like to wear men's clothes, keeping a husband close in the glimpses they catch of themselves: they have no other way to reach one. I might as well do the same.

With no one but me to find it, my body is meaningless. There's no reason for it any more. I walk about and know that I'm holding this heat, my own heat, this turning, this shine of what I am and the sweet skin hidden somewhere and the truth, the softness of truth, the peace of me. And of course no one here sees it—why would I show it to them? I would rather waste it, do waste it, there's nothing else it will allow. It's burying itself in beyond what I can touch. Or let anyone touch.

"We have some very fine animals today, I'm sure you'll agree. Next bull out will be Napalm. That's Derry MacKay, riding Napalm."

A dark slab of shoulder shuddered behind the gate. Above, there came a flicker of bright yellow from a shirt, a rising hand in a pale glove.

Trying with Freddie, that finished it. Finished me.

It hadn't surprised her: sliding to the end of a night at the bar, starting to gather up glasses, and Freddie sitting by himself and easy the way he always would be: easy and meaningless. She'd said what she had to, smiled as she ought, her timing out

and no sensation in it, but that made no difference to Freddie—
too drunk to tell.

But she wasn't surprised, only cold, a little sick.

I wanted to prove that I still could. I wanted to prove I was alive.
Stumbling along outside, understanding that she would be
numb by the time she reached her house. Freddie's hands already
sliding, jabbing, making everything a theft. There was no more
permission she could give.

He would have hauled her down before she'd opened her
door, he would have liked that, leaning a hard whisky sweat at
her back and pushing while she rushed the lock.

It didn't work.

Then they fell in the hall and she was lying under him, dry
as ash, while he tried to force it, while he mumbled baby-talk,
tried again, swore. And she wasn't numb: she could feel every
part of the stain of him, his animal weight.

Where I end up, my last resort.

She clawed and scrambled free, her knee catching him, ran
with her shoes off, her blouse half undone, the clasp on her skirt
broken, locked herself in the bathroom until he'd hammered and
yelled and then laughed himself tired, until he'd kicked the front
door wide and gone.

*That'll be his story of me now, that I froze, that I ran away. My
fault entirely.*

The bull slammed out sideways, raised a wall of driven dust,
plunged out through it, the yellow shirt above, tick-jerking back
and forth easily, quickly, like something trivial. And, ratcheting,
the man dropped to the animal's flank, unseated, hung by his
hand, dragged, and then almost appeared to shrug or dance into
a twist, a confusion, an unlikely snap of the head.

I can make love. I have love to make.

June saw the rodeo clown leap out and caper the bull away

while two men, three, leaped down into the ring and ran to kneel around the man's body, where it lay very flat and surprisingly straight on the sand, something red across its face. A tiny ambulance bumped in through the far gate.

"We're going to give them all the time they need, ladies and gentlemen, to do what they have to before they take him off to hospital."

Forty-five minutes away, that's the nearest hospital.

Two paramedics in jumpsuits were working at MacKay now, they'd brought out a stretcher, the gleam of equipment incongruous in the filth of the arena. And a long-limbed boy in a big hat and a bright yellow shirt like his father's was sitting up on the fence, leaning forward, a man beside him, resting one hand on his shoulder—perhaps to comfort, perhaps to restrain. And, as if she had wished herself there, a woman was out in the ring now, pretty in snug jeans, a silk blouse, tawny hair, and pushing at one of the cowboys and nodding her head, please, please, please, and then turning her back on the benches, curling over at the waist to make some kind of privacy, because clearly she couldn't bear to be here with everybody watching and clearly she also couldn't leave.

"We'll let you know as soon as we hear anything, folks. Just as soon as we hear."

The ambulance rocked away in silence, not a hint of its engine, only a dumb progression through the gate and on to the track and then joining the first, grey curve of the road. It seemed the pressure of so many eyes must have taken away its sound.

Forty-five minutes and where will God be when they get there.

The arena was cleared when June looked round to it again. Beyond the rise, cars would be leaving to follow the ambulance. She turned and walked with her back to the sun until she reached a steep bank, the grass tall on it, but flattened out into smoothed forms wherever somebody had sat or lain during the day, the wider areas where there'd been couples, or families. June picked out an unmarked spot for herself and sat, liking the press of stems around her. Another few weeks and this would be dried to straw.

Out of sight now, the rodeo continued: what sounded like laughter and drifted cheers as the pack race started: a mule bray, more laughs. June shut her eyes and saw the woman in the ring and the way she nodded, all of her movements jagged with terror, struggling under the first rise of pain.

And I was the only one there, the only ugly, wrong one who wanted that, just that. I have no sympathy for her, or compassion, no interest: I only want the right to be so injured, to know what I miss. To have someone I can lose.

I only want a reason for the sadness. Please, God, I do. Let me hurt for the sake of a body I've loved, a body that loved me. Please, God, only that.

She didn't know if she was crying, whether anyone could see, and the clouds dragged over the evening hills in silence and there was nothing left for her to burn.

White House at Night

Danny wondered where he was: where *he* was. Really—which was the place in the body where he felt himself to be.

It was something that you did know—you just never thought of it. Ask the question and the answer always came: "I'm up here, mainly up here," with yourself inside this little kind of capsule, busy at the back of your eyes and aiming wherever they aimed: quieter with them shut, but definitely in there all the time, huddled in some indefinable space at the back of your sinuses and arched up, somehow, over the roof of your mouth, an invisible lodger.

You could feel through the whole of your body, you were aware it belonged to you and was personal, but *you—where you were*—that didn't quite extend into your limbs, it faded. There was a sense of attention lying in your hands, maybe, in your prick, but truly you were in your head, that was where you lived.

He knew the experiment, thought he remembered it from a lecture—where you'd ask someone to write their own name on their forehead and almost every time they wrote it backwards, for the benefit of this interior self they had, crouched behind their face, seeing out through their skull.

That proved it—everyone lived inside their heads.

So when Niamh said that as a criticism of him, she was wrong. His living there only meant that he was human and she didn't understand. He was just a human being, like everyone else.

At some point, the sun had set and now the room was wavering with passing headlamps, the bigger gleam of trams, then resting in darkness and dry warmth. The heating was great here, defying the evening's frost with faultless, Swiss efficiency. In fact, it wasn't a bad place, all round—much cleaner and much larger than the one they had to use, out by the pit.

Imre had said they could go off and stay here as long as they wanted. "Take. Take. An apartment of my highly good friend in Lucerne. He never is at home," Imre had insisted. "Quiet place, Lucerne. You will enjoy." Of course, they wouldn't *have* as long as they wanted, they never did. "Is very . . . very tidy. Not like here. Take."

One day to get there—the truck and then two planes could do it—one day to come back, but then four free for them to stay: four pristine days somewhere else. It made sense to accept the offer, the keys, the scrawling map with a jagged blur of lake shaded in pencil. "Quiet place." Even if it indebted them to Imre. "Niamh will like such a place—you will see." Even then. "Make her happy." They'd needed a rest and this would be it. "Take. You should take."

They hadn't quite shaken the pit, though. It stayed with them: with him, Dan supposed that would be more accurate. He still had the peat smell on his hands and that other, deeper scent, or the memory of it, would rise in him when he relaxed: butyric acid, methane, sometimes a faint tang like metal and what he could only think of as the taste of unreality, of a situation it would never be possible to accept, even when you were in it: perhaps most especially then. The particular mix of odours was universal: death announcing itself quite predictably on any continent.

This time the preservation had been good, the bodies buried quickly in a wet, acidic soil—ideal conditions and quite unusual for this terrain. Theoretically, the chances of identification were high: some of the faces stained, but not overly altered, some clothing perhaps recognisable. Amongst a few of those found in the lower layers, fingerprints were not out of the question, the pliant skin coaxed into gloving away from hands, almost intact. A relatively simple matter, in such cases, to trim off what he needed and ease a finger inside each dead sheath, set each blued nail above one of his own, dip himself into the shadow of another man. A layer of latex between them, of course—hygiene. He would ink up then, careful, press and roll the necessary print. Niamh did the same for the women whenever that proved appropriate. Children were more difficult, small: but then, unless they'd been printed as infants and records could be found, there wasn't much point in trying, anyway.

Down in the current pit there were fifty-three bodies, so far—back home, he might not see that many in a year. Seventeen at the last site, a messy reburial, dusted with lime. Ninety-eight in the grave before that. It was a wonderful opportunity to learn.

It was wonderful, too, that Niamh could be here with him. She always seemed to worry about safety, which was not unreasonable—the people who buried the corpses were multiple murderers, they wanted the soil to absolve them of their crimes and they wanted you to leave things be. In Chile, in Argentina and now here, you were a disturbance they'd rather avoid. This made for risks, of course it did, and Niamh was a woman who liked to have certainties.

There were times when they'd watched him digging, he knew—the murderers. They'd look on with this odd expression, almost coquettish, almost proud, and quietly disbelieving that anyone would actually try and retrieve the irretrievable: scraping up no more than proof of annihilation, when it had never been particularly secret, only the kind of joke that sensible people denied having heard. Those intended for destruction had been destroyed—what more could one want to know? What more could there be?

Danny worked while they tilted their heads and puzzled over the string grids and the little, coloured flags, the expensive cameras—all the fussing paraphernalia of his job—and he knew it must seem inadequate. He was supposed to be here to unearth justice, give the dead their voice—but all the dead could ever do was list their injuries, confirm the absolute success of their tormentors. Nothing Danny did had any *strength*, he knew.

And so did they, the watchers, they could taste his doubt. When they caught his eye, they would start a smile, teasing, ready for him to give some sign of his real motives: he must have motives, his own variety of guilt. The whole thing made him ashamed and then angry with himself. He was meant to be doing a good thing, so he ought to feel good, he ought to be able to manage that. Arresting those responsible would help. It hardly ever happened, though.

Possibly that was why the murderers never seemed ashamed, or angry—very seldom even made a threat—or not that he'd heard of. The ones who threatened were the bereaved: calling down vengeance, tugging out sudden, battered guns: defending their own, months too late.

Which Niamh should never be involved with, not any of it—she was right. So he'd tended to come out alone in the past, but on this trip they were well protected—UN troops and local bodyguards. He'd persuaded her that it was safe, because it was important they should be together. They did the same work and they ought to be doing it in the same place.

He stood, walked across and looked down from the window.

The Casino glowed discreetly opposite: a long, neat block in pastel orange and cream: no neon, nobody entering or leaving, no sign of anyone trying to take a risk. For a moment, he pressed his cheek against the dull cool of the glass and then drew back. He raised his hands to the top of his head, spread his fingers over it, then gripped, as if he might feel a movement inside, might surprise the shiver of himself if he could only squeeze down hard enough.

Nothing.

Danny bent to remove his shoes and socks. His jacket was already somewhere on the floor. He'd put on a tie when he'd still been planning to go out and eat, but he wouldn't need it now: so off it came, then dropped.

The bereaved—he pulled his shirt free of his waistband and knew he was going to remember them. No use telling them not to come—they did what they wanted, moved with this awful kind of privilege.

They were the same in every country. Quite often, no one should know when a pit was opened, but they'd arrive in any case, get closer than they should: the ones who shouted, the ones who stood, the ones who had never done this before, the ones who now did nothing else. The ones who wept.

All the ways human beings can weep—he'd begun to learn the variations and realised that they were virtually infinite, as characteristic as dental work, or DNA.

Its buttons being done with, he removed his shirt, balled it up and threw it towards a corner, didn't hear it land.

The ones left behind, they had photographs, descriptions of people who weren't people any more—the hobbies, the small things the dead had enjoyed. Fathers and brothers arrived quite regularly, but mainly women came, particularly mothers, less frequently wives. He told every one of them to leave: register details, perhaps pay respects, say goodbye, but leave. The pits were never anything they should see.

One tug and his belt pulled loose with a slapping glide and he could swing it, intending to let it fall, but then he reconsidered and kept his grip. He clutched the buckle and started to circle his arm, across his body and then out wide, the leather thrumming and turning silent in a cycle, as if there were someone else with him here, drawing shuddered breaths.

Backing into the dim centre of the room, he turned slowly, still swinging, and knocked over an ornament of some kind—heavy china—then another—he thought the Venetian glass fish. Then he regathered his momentum while he listened to something tumble, roll and break satisfyingly. He slashed down at the table next, cracking his belt over the glimmer of the bonbon dish and his whisky glass. Then he ran, flailing, cutting across his own shins, making contact with the chair where he'd been sitting and lashing it, meaning the strokes, intending the injury implied by every arc.

When he stopped he felt ragged, jarred. He set down the belt, unfastened his trousers, bent to hurry them down, his underpants, too, his socks, and then he stepped clear. It was time to go up to the window again, enjoy its length, his bare feet nervous of broken glass on the carpet, but not so nervous that he didn't walk. When he reached the view—the single, high pane—he was still unharmed.

He braced his legs and eased forward, a smooth chill ready to meet him from his forehead to his knees, his chest and stomach pushing sharp against the window, relenting, then pushing again. Danny hadn't realised he was breathless, hadn't noticed an effort in what he'd done. His cock stung with the cold, but it barely disturbed him: he tucked his hips forward, squeezed the bite clear back into his balls, and then lifted his arms, stretched them up along the glass, his palms set flat above. He turned his head to one side, made his fit closer and gave himself up. The street noise sounded hollow and very distant.

But no one was going to notice him. This was calm and pretty Switzerland: no one would look up.

Although they ought to, because he deserved it. A shame to drive out a shame that should make him feel good, please him.

This afternoon, he'd stood at the lakeside, leaned over the rail beside Niamh, and they'd watched as the coots disappeared themselves under the surface, swam through the greenish clarity of water, their backs silvered over with clinging air, heads purposeful. They'd popped to the surface again, neat and unscathed, white beaks occupied with morsels of something. They were very pleasing. The tufted ducks, the swans, the wooden bridges: all very pleasing. They just hadn't pleased him.

He'd excused himself and found a call box, phoned Conrad and asked about body 41. It was female and unusual—both breasts augmented with implants. They'd discovered her lying on her side, the implant gels already drifted into the peat close by her torso: soft and incongruous, like something marine. They'd traced the manufacturer and make: Style 186, round saline implant with anterior diaphragm valve and an RTV silicone elastomer textured shell. They had the catalogue, lot and serial numbers on a woman's hope of change, her idea of beauty, maybe, personal confidence.

"Bonnie Dukic." Conrad had the name ready.

"OK." The name didn't mean a thing to Danny, of course, and she was dead now, she didn't need it. "Relatives?"

"In the States. I think in the States—born there, Bonnie Simic. Married one Hasim Dukic and went back to the old country. They had a son, Aleksandar." There was no reason to suggest that either her husband or son were still alive.

"Well. A name, then. Good."

"I could have told you this when you got back."

"Yes." Danny often enjoyed hearing Conrad—there was a tranquillity about him.

"You're on holiday, Dan. Remember." He could be overly moral, superior, but most of the time he would just ask questions and let you realise your answers told you how you should proceed.

"Yes." Danny had wanted to be more forthcoming, but he'd felt hot, unsteady.

"Niamh enjoying it?" He would let you accuse yourself, Conrad—that was his drawback, his problem.

"Both of us are. Yes. Should get back to it, in fact." Conrad hadn't answered, leaving a friendly silence when Danny had no need for friendliness. "See you on Monday."

"Take it easy."

"Of course."

Danny had wondered if Aleksandar was the boy in the carrier bag. Number 15. It wouldn't be very difficult to work out: the mother's DNA leading on to the son, the son's perhaps finding them the father.

He'd gone back to the railing and hugged Niamh, her body lighting against him, feeling happy, and then drifting, turning wooden until he let her go. Or perhaps that had been his fault, perhaps he'd seemed cold, somehow, and had made her colder.

That kind of thing, the game-playing, it tired him. It left him wondering what clothes Niamh would be wearing when they found her. In the end, the absolute end, you were always an object to be discovered, sometimes straightforward, sometimes not. Or she could be naked: what was intended might come and take her when she was like that. Yes, she might be naked.

Danny realised he was used to the window, couldn't feel it any more. He could imagine it had disappeared and left him supported purely by a type of will, a resistance beyond his control. The way that he lived now, this wouldn't seem surprising. Like when he was going to the pit, there was a path to take—secure and cleared of mines—but some mornings he couldn't use it, he would have to push up through the woods, hysteria cramping in his calf muscles and his whole shirt sweated through with the terror of stepping on something bad. Still, that was the way he had to go.

He shifted his weight and the pattern of cold changed across his stomach. A creak eased out left along the window frame. Danny thought he heard a laugh break from the street. Panic flared in his chest, but he stayed where he was, displayed. He had no choice.

He was beginning to believe that no one did. Staying awake late, packed in the kitchen with Imre and the guards: "They're shits." He said all the things that he couldn't tell Conrad: "They do it because they can." He let go of his secrets. "Human beings like to know what they can. Like to do it."

"Yes. Of course. Yes." Imre, grinning. He liked it when Danny was drunk and when it was dark: he always got more friendly then, more interested.

"They fucking love it." The guards didn't speak English, or didn't seem to. Imre, when he wanted, could also pretend not to understand. "Love. It. Bastards." With them, Danny could relax, as if he was speaking to no one, and he could say everything—even those thoughts which would prove unacceptable, if voiced in a humanitarian group. "Like sex—think how much of that's in you, how much you want that—they love it like that."

"Sex? You know about this, Mr. Dan?" Imre needling for some reason, alert and ducking away, giggling.

"I said . . . I said the way they love it . . ."

And then formal, leaning forward, brisk, "Did you think it

was something else, Mr. Dan? Money?—everyone loves this, frankly, yes—and to take some farm, some house you wanted for a long time—this is good. But killing, you have to love—just to kill, not to get something. To kill like this . . . you love." Imre had rested a hand on Danny's shoulder, "You understand." The touching hungry, overly firm.

And Danny did, he understood. Conrad excused actions, he blurred the truth with lectures about propaganda, paranoia, political manipulation of the innocent. He praised the essential nature of humanity. Everyone pretended they agreed. But Danny knew, could feel, the essential nature of humanity, its real self, whenever he stood in the pit—that's where it was. Then he could taste the murderers, their love. Conrad was like a child. He was very noble and admirable and a good, if pedantic, teacher, but he was still a child.

"No one stop them . . ." Imre sipped at his vodka gently, "then they go on. They go on for ever." His drinking was always controlled. "It is made for them." He brought in the vodka once a week, took orders and hard currency: sold cigarettes, too, chocolate, condoms, tinned milk, Christ knew what else. "They are made for it."

Danny bought nothing.

Nothing but condoms.

Alone in somebody else's expensive apartment, Danny tasted Imre's voice and stretched, keeping position, his skin clinging to the glass, adhering, used to its place. Still, there was an ache between his shoulders that he had to stop. He couldn't tell how long he'd need to stay this way and he didn't want to hurt more than he had to.

The necessary time would pass while he balanced inside his head, the way everyone did, doing or avoiding what they had to and watching the results. Human beings were built this way.

They could only lose so much blood, only stand so much pain, only function within a defined range of abuse, and everyone had their own patterns of resistance. One individual might dodge what was intended, another might lean against it, and others might let it drive them along. The happiest would be driven, their whole lives effortless. They would have the space and energy to appreciate pleasing things.

The condoms, for instance: in Chile, in Argentina, here: he bought condoms. He needed them. They were intended for him. Because there were always women without their husbands, without their children, pain stiff in their clothes like blood, and some of those women were also intended for him.

Watch the angle of her hands, the way tiredness slows her, the collapse of everything but loneliness—it's a kind of decay and you know about decay—and you walk towards her—like you walk in the dangerous woods—and you speak to her in words she may not understand, but softly, kindly, and she knows she has to go with you, because this is a part of her life's shape: this is how it is.

Pulling one down in the trees, behind the tents, or risking her in your accommodation, or finally, naturally, drawing one over beside what the night shows of a pit—whichever pit—and then having her angry beneath you, or like meat, or taking you for someone else. It was intended.

Everything he did was inevitable, but he wasn't strong, he never could fully let himself surrender to that part of being human. He stayed anxious, he struggled, and this was why he felt bad instead of forgetting his reservations in the shine of limbs, rucked cloth, the bared clench of their teeth.

His prick thickened against the pane, knowing how it should be: held within the perfect limit, making him unforgiving as bone and driving, finding their heat. The women made him hard because he should be.

But not this trip.

Imre had handed over the first packs solemnly, knowingly, "Trojan brand. For the lovely wife." Saying this as if it were not offensive. "Marriage a noble estate, yes, Mr. Dan?" His face impassive now, even bored.

Danny grabbing the package, mumbling, "Yes." Because he hadn't thought of Niamh, he'd bought out of habit and now he realised, "Yes." Niamh used a diaphragm. "That's right." They didn't want children.

So, while she was busy, down in the mortuary tent, Danny stole Niamh's diaphragm. Then he threw it, along with its case, into the river. He also took a bracelet and her wedding ring—she never wore them to work—and those he buried beside a hedge. She found the thefts disturbing, but not unlikely. Danny offered her friendly silence.

Niamh still didn't like the thought of condoms, they seemed cheap, she said, they reminded her of disease.

Danny coaxed, persuaded, pretended a lack of practice when he rolled the first one on. And they did make love, because they were meant to, but she didn't bare her teeth for him and she didn't forget who he was. He tried to like it.

"Ah, Mr. Danny . . . So serious always."

It hadn't been such a surprise when Imre turned up in Lucerne. "So serious, but such a pleasure."

They'd walked out of the café, Danny and Niamh together, heading towards the Water Tower and there had been Imre, crossing the road to meet them, not at all as if he'd stood and waited for them, but with his timing so exact that he must have done. "Such pleasure."

The only other way to be so right, so properly placed in time, was to give yourself over completely to your intentions. Imre who travelled too much to be honest, who made too much money, who had at least one other name—Ivo something, Ivo

Hemon—Imre who might have done terrible things, you could tell he understood intention and how to be pleased by humanity.

"You have had lunch?"

Niamh nodded and Imre faked a frown, nudging in beside her.

"Then I will ask you both to have dinner at my expense. Fish. Perhaps fish?"

And then they had strolled, as if this had been arranged, beside the *quais* and Imre had brought out a bag of stale bread, gulls mewing as soon as it left the pocket of his overcoat. "If you will allow . . . ?" his eyebrows raised to Danny, confirming permission, rather than asking it and his arm steering Niamh over the gravel pathway, to the fat stones at the lakeside and then the water and the jostle of gathered birds. They'd bent, side by side, Danny a few feet behind them, and Imre had offered the bag and Niamh had scattered out the crumbs, as if this were their ideal configuration, the one that nature had favoured all along. Imre and Niamh, hands making no contact—the rhythm forming perfectly between them without a touch.

It had never occurred to Danny that if he could fuck other people, so could she. Fancy that. It seemed obvious now.

The bread finished, Niamh had dusted off her palms and fingers, then brushed briefly at Imre's—his skin being an extension of her own. She hadn't paused after, hadn't even thought to blush, only returned to her husband, smiling, assured.

"See this, Mr. Dan? We feed the swans, we feed the ducks and then tonight we will eat ourselves. Everything has its turn, yes?"

And Danny had given him his only possible answer, "Yes," and felt the rush of purpose round him, irresistible. The human beings who had purpose, the ones who could hold it, ride it, they could take anything they wanted from anyone.

Niamh would be with Imre now: Imre had brought them

both here for that. Danny had spent years digging, examining, trying to believe that he was working for what was right, was helping to make what was right become clear. But what was right was this—was this here—this man was supposed to fuck his wife, Imre was supposed to fuck Niamh, and he was supposed to not be in their way.

He'd been invited to the dinner, but he wasn't meant to accept—it was his place to make things simple. And, anyway, he couldn't have moved himself through the front door if he'd tried—too much resistance.

Staying here, this was his purpose—what he had to do—it was human and necessary for him to keep braced against the glass and ready, pointlessly naked, for when Niamh might come back—perhaps with Imre, perhaps not.

She ought to be the one to notice him, she ought to look up.

He didn't know what should happen after that.

A Wrong Thing

I would prefer not to open my eyes, not this morning. In the end, I know I'll have to, but I'll do it against my will. I would much rather not co-operate.

And the insects, they don't help. They're outside, I've no clue how many, but apparently a lot, and all of them are making these hot, unpredictable scuttles of noise: like loosed wires sparking, like tin toys breaking up: there beyond the walls and windows, thousands of tiny instincts signalling they want to kill each other and have sex.

That's fine, though, because they're not in here with me, at least I don't think so. I have no desire to check.

But I would like to know why my mouth tastes of rust, which means iron, which means blood. I hope I've just eaten rust and forgotten about it; hardly likely, but I'll try to think so, anyway. Last night, I must have swallowed something rusty, or licked it, and now I don't recall, can't yet recall. And I think I had a dream with metal in it: perhaps it's possible to save a flavour you've known in your sleep.

I have definitely saved a bad feeling of some kind, another aftertaste, and both of my eyes are still shut, because I am nervous about them being any other way.

Even so, it will be OK, not unpleasant, completely familiar, when I break out into my first look at the day. I can do that: it isn't a threat, shouldn't be a threat, there shouldn't be anything untoward about it.

Shuttered windows, slicing jabs of light, the bed beneath me bobbing briefly like a dinghy on a lazy sea. Which is wrong, definitely.

There you are, though, seeing—no problem, nothing to worry about.

Except for the bed and the light, which is far advanced, the kind that you only get when you've missed the morning and I didn't think I had. It also hurts, which it really shouldn't. Deep in the meat of my brain, something I can't identify has become extremely sensitive and, tucked away beneath all this, my teeth feel unfamiliar and my tongue is, somehow, in the way.

My bed bobs again.

I wish it wouldn't.

But this is not a problem: it is a solution, in fact, because now I understand the bobbing, the bad feeling, the trouble with my eyes, the rust: I am not well.

I am not well and in a foreign country.

So I should think about insurance and if I took any out and what class I might come under—negligence, poisoning, infection, act of God—I'm not exactly sure how I will qualify.

I don't want to see a doctor.

I'm almost certain that I dreamed about a doctor, one I didn't like. Sleeping or waking, there's no way to tell here if someone truly *is* a doctor, if their needles are clean, or necessary, if what they say they'll do to you is safe. So I'll go without.

But I am in a foreign country and sick.

My legs are sticking to the sheets, I notice, everything about me showing obvious signs of being overheated, feverish.

Nice word, feverish. You couldn't guess its meaning.

I did think I was cold, but apparently I'm not. Skin under sweat, it's meant to look attractive. It doesn't—it blotches and drags, seems furtive, unclean.

This will be the photograph they use, post mortem—distasteful areas boxed out under black—and then there'll be the holiday snap— here she is, when still living—the unwittingly poignant smile. The papers will show them both for contrast. Or maybe I'll only make it to the internet, uncensored.

Anyway, I don't have a holiday snap. I don't take them. I don't want to see and no one else does, either.

A pressure fingers underneath my heart and my mouth fills with saliva. Swallowing is difficult and doesn't help, I have to wipe my lips which I find are now oily and vaguely obscene. I reach behind my head, unsteadying the edges, the corners, the meeting places of the ceiling, walls, floor. I catch at the air conditioner's control and turn it. The mechanism jolts and then begins to grind out a minor disturbance in the padded warmth above my face. Without intending, I picture vast wheels milling, hidden by the plasterboard, crushing the limbs of something, wet tufts of hair, lodged and oozing in the cogs.

No, imagine nice things, kind things, happy things, cool water, cut grass.

Frost. Frost on a field: a meadow, better word, meadow: and a little, frozen river under trees, well-intentioned trees.

The pace of my saliva relents and the weight in my stomach shifts, sly, but then settles, not unbearable.

I could lie on the river, roll out flat, naked, cheek to cheek.

I have a clear, soothing sense of frozen water, the slowly melting nubs and flats of it, moulding to me, and my panic is resting back, dwindling, until the idea of ice reopens last night's dream.

I was ill there, too: in a hotel room, a bathroom, the bathroom I have now: grubby white tiling walls, truncated tub, everything the

*same. Trying to sit up in the bath and the ice chips sinking under-
neath me, creaking when they shift, lifting my hands which are thick
with cold crystals, brownish pink.*

The mirror opposite me seems to fluctuate and pitch. I may
have brain damage. I may be hallucinating. I may already be
entirely unable to tell which.

Then I hold still and everything else does, too.

*Somebody told me this, or I read it: the story where you wake up
in an ice bath and, taped where you can see, there's a note which says
you shouldn't stand, shouldn't even try to, that everything is over and
done with, no point in being alarmed.*

"Good evening. Service."

Out in the corridor, a pass key fidgets at the lock.

Good evening, what?

Louder, "Good evening. Service," the door sweeping open
and, almost immediately, jolting to a stop. I've left on the security
chain—being a nervous traveller comes in handy, now and then.

*What time is it, though—I mean the real time? The staff here say
the same thing to anyone English-speaking, night or day. Here it's
both good and an evening perpetually.*

"Service."

I'm going to start bleeding somewhere, if he keeps up that noise.

"Come back." I have to swallow again. "Later." My voice
sounding masculine and strangled. "Please."

"Service, good evening." The door nudges in again experi-
mentally, but gets no further.

What the hell is "Service," anyway?

"I am not well. Come back. Tomorrow." My stomach cramps
slightly, teasing.

He'll understand "tomorrow," surely to God.

"I clean room now, please." The voice doesn't sound insis-
tent, only certain of how things are done.

"No. You clean tomorrow. TO-MOR-ROW."

God, I sound like a racist. Bellowing things, demanding. I mean, I respect other cultures, I try, but I do only have this one language, which is a failing, but what can I do. I want to sound agreeable, that is completely what I intend.

"Service. I clean today."

"OH, WILL YOU JUST *FUCK OFF!*"

Jesus, I'm sorry, I'm absolutely sorry, I totally am.

There is a wounded silence in which I do not audibly apologise. *Well, I didn't ask for "Service."* Then the door flinches shut, the lock clacks, and I don't feel remotely relieved because of this kicking which blossoms through my torso, and raises a fresh, throbbing sweat. If I don't reach the bathroom before I exhale, I will vomit in my bed.

Funny how you always want your mother when you're throwing up. No matter what.

Funny.

And let's do this properly, first time—clear and finished, please. Get rid of the lot.

So think of the note, the dream of the note—

You see yourself, you're shivering and reading that surgeons have taken out both of your kidneys, they've drugged you and stolen the pair, and then sewn you up, empty and dying and packed round with bloodstained ice. You haven't been murdered, your body will kill you: slowly, because you've been chilled.

Oh, dear God.

And this works like a nasty charm, clears more than everything. While I shake through the last, hard coughs I move my hands to check my unaltered back. I'm still complete.

Tim was there in my sleep, too. I remember now, seeing him turn his head, as if I'd called. He was sheepish and excited, at the edge of smiling: the way he'd always be while he waited to see if I knew that he'd done a wrong thing: when he wanted to check we were both going to like it, make it allowed.

My throat feels ragged. But the spasms have turned drowsy and subsided: I do seem better.

I finish the last of the bottled water, rinsing my mouth and then sipping. *Avoid dehydration—it creeps up.* Beyond the windows, I hear thin, repeated screams from what I guess must be a bird, something anxious and predatory, ascending to my left. Walking evenly, as if I might spill, I go back to the wreck of my bed and then lie down gently.

Tim would have enjoyed this.

Not that Tim welcomed illness for itself, he just wanted to take care. It's what pleased him: padding about with aspirin, hot-water bottles, snacks.

He would take off his glasses and we would understand that I was just better enough. He would take off his glasses and put them beside the lamp, pull the covers back. He would take off his glasses and blink, be free then to lower his head, his clever mouth.

I am breathing through my teeth, trying to keep the memory angled away and to have no feeling. This isn't a time when I can afford to be disturbed.

Sometimes I would just pretend, go upstairs and draw the curtains, fighting fit and waiting for his mouth.

This is unwise. This is not a time to think.

When Tim was ill himself, though, he preferred to be left alone— like a cat, he said. Then I found him on a Sunday morning, early, in the kitchen, and I told him he didn't have flu, that it was serious, and then the first doctor finally arrived and talked to me as if I was a child, said house calls were reserved for emergencies, but after that, Tim was trying to walk and falling and talking, shouting, at nobody, and then I made a second doctor come, with an ambulance on its way, because I'd described Tim's rash again and made them understand that he had meningitis and might die.

Might die.

But I knew he wouldn't.

They shaved his head and trepanned him to let the pressure out. In three places, they drilled through his skull and he was alone with them when they did it. But, when it was finished, I sat by his bed, stayed there talking, saying his name for days while he was still. I kept calling him in. I was sure he wouldn't go, that he couldn't leave me.

He came home two stone lighter and with a soft haze of regrowth on his scalp, a dressing, tape. And he had a new skin: fierce and pale and naked, completely naked. I couldn't see him without touching him. At first, only with my mouth, because that was gentle. He needed gentleness.

I move my head to study the telephone; like the rest of the room, it is behaving normally. I could use it to call Tim. The time difference, though, the other differences—it would all end up being too difficult.

While he lay on the hospital bed, I made him promises, more than I can remember, I put all that we might be into his silence, his sleep. Sometimes I think it's made me seem an anticlimax to him since—I never have lived up to any of the dreams I gave him—he settled for second best by coming back to life.

I roll on my side and set the walls and carpet swinging, my head is muzzled suddenly, held in something wet. I retch, stumble up for the bathroom and retch again.

When I kneel, I don't touch the toilet—*no need to volunteer for other illnesses*—I breathe between the rising cramps—*Oh Jesus, oh Jesus Christ*—and again I want my mother. *Fuck.* Another series of jolts. *Oh, fuck it.*

And nothing happens, not a thing. In what must be half an hour, I bring up a single, scouring mouthful of bile. Whatever this is, I can't be rid of it.

Back on the bed, I crouch, defensive, suddenly burning, and reach for the phone. In a quite unlikely but persuasive way, it seems both more beautiful and more solid than it did before:

a worryingly lovely, heavy telephone with a button to press for messages—*I either haven't got one, or it doesn't work*—and one for reception and one with a symbol I don't recognise—*God knows*—and one with a miniature waiter holding a miniature tray—*which means Room Service. Not "Service."* **Room Service**—*that's what I want.*

"Yes, Room Service? I need water. Please." *I have no water left.* "Large-sized bottle; bottles. I want two large-sized bottles of water." *Without it, a person can die.*

The line out to wherever Room Service is prickles and whines.

"The biggest size."

I have no idea if I am audible, or understood. "I have not been well." *As if they care.* "Sorry . . . Can you?—Sorry. Water . . . Water?"

There must be guests who can do this, who find it easy, who can just order things. "Sorry. Two bottles. Please." *Without making a single apology. Or saying please.* "Two bottles . . . Hello? Good evening?"

The connection oozes away, implacably uncommunicative, and finishes with a little click.

If Room Service never arrives, there will be no water. I need water. If Room Service **does** *arrive, there* **will** *be water. Which I need. But then I will have to get dressed and stand up and unlock the door and reach out and get the water, carry it.*

I don't know if I can.

Now, even when I close my eyes, something undulates—the blood light at the back of my eyelids, it's treacherous. If Tim was here I would tell him about it, or would have told him, before the meningitis and the disappointment.

It was that time, that evening, weekday evening, when I walked in on him and watched his face close, everything blurring to neutral, to a chill, just because I was there. I had surprised him being the way that he used to be, but it wasn't for me any more, so he shut it away.

We spend more time working, he takes evenings out, it surprises me now when we meet in the house; going into a quiet room and there he'll be. I try to look irritated and leave before he does. We go on holiday separately.

I flatten myself to the sheet, press and press my forehead against the small creak of the mattress as if this will alter a single mistake I've made. Because I didn't shout, didn't grab him by the arm and shout in his face, didn't throw a clock I was fond of and hurt to see it smashed and to see him keep on going, leave the room without a sound—I didn't do any of that until it was only stupid and too late. An infection in the brain, the doctors told me, might make him different and so I went against myself and drifted for months, let him be, let what I knew of him leave me.

Except when that light comes back to his skin, that nakedness. Not to talk, not to see each other—it's only to meet his mouth, lace my hands behind his new, cropped hair, know we can taste what hasn't changed.

"Room Service, good evening."

The door stammers with a series of knocks and I am caught in the cold recollection of lying beneath a husband I can't speak to, both of us dead weights, breathing, recovering ourselves, our sadness, our embarrassment.

"Room Service, good evening."

"Yes." I am still naked. "Yes. Good evening." And I don't want to move. "Leave it outside the door." I don't want anyone near me.

"You want—?" It isn't the would-be room cleaner, I think I would recognise that voice.

"I said, leave it outside the door." *And if I sound like a Colonial oppressor, I don't care.* "I CAN'T GET UP NOW. LEAVE IT."

"Good evening. Thank you." This sounds slightly put out, but a muffled clunking gives me cause for hope.

I will stand, I will wrap myself up in the sheet and do what I must to get my water.

When my hand finds the child-skin at the small of his back, I always wait for that.

My scalp tingles, as if there were someone behind me, or above, and the insects worry on and I lever up to sit, then stand. My balance swims, but lands again and I drag the sheet round to cover me, shuffle for the door.

The lock foxes me for a moment, no more than that, I open it, lean out into the hot, empty passageway, swipe down for the two bottles, retrieve them and half stagger back. The effort of this bangs in my head. Still, I have my water—that's fine.

"Good evening. Good evening? Room Service?"

The line is a little worse than before, as if it anticipated my call and is already disapproving.

"Yes. I ordered water. Two bottles of water and you left them." If anyone is listening, they make no sound. "Someone left them . . ." *This is too complicated.* "Someone left them and I have them, but the seals on the bottles are broken . . ." I wait for an intervention of some kind, but none is forthcoming: I will have to say this all on my own. "If the seals are broken . . . by mistake." *There's no reason to accuse anybody—obviously that's what I'm doing, but I don't really mean it that way.* "I can't drink. I have been ill. All day ill. I need clean water."

"Our water is clean."

"I'll . . ." *Shit.* "Look, I'll pay for new bottles, but if the seals—"

"I will send him again." The distant receiver clanks down.

So I'll have to be ready when he arrives.

Shit.

I move to look at my jeans where they're crumpled on the chair, moderately baffling, and then lift them, scattering meaningless small coins out of the pockets, a crush of dirty notes. Methodically, I balance, step, waver, then work my way in. The T-shirt is easier. After that, I stay on the chair, waiting, smoothing my breath, ducking every thought of Tim's hands, the way they can be, confident with fastenings, the parting drift of cloth.

More quickly than I expected, the knock comes.

"You have a problem." He is perhaps seventeen, lost in somebody's oversized guess at an impressive uniform: cuffed black trousers, a purple jacket with gold piping, creased patent leather shoes. "There is something wrong." He makes each statement critical and precise, a slight edge there to emphasise that he can understand my language while I would be lost in his.

Well, I'll apologise for being British later.

"I, ah, yes. The seals . . ." *This sounds so petty.* "I'm sure this has nothing to do with you, maybe your supplier . . ." *His sleeves are turned under to fit—and he sees that I've noticed.*

He sets down two new bottles of water on the table and lifts up the old, unwilling to admit defeat. "The seals . . . ?" He delicately twists both caps, then waits, surveying primly, making it plain that he dislikes me, the tangled bed, the slovenly room, the indications of deeper disorder.

I try to sound brisk. "The seals are broken, as you can see." *I should have put on underwear—then I might have a sense of authority.* "That will be all."

"Our supplier is at fault. I am so sorry." This in an insincere drawl.

I will have to sit down soon. "That's fine, then." The young man shows no sign of moving.

Well, I'm not giving him a tip—not unless it makes him go away.

His hands are shaking visibly. I suppose that he might be afraid, either furious or afraid, perhaps both.

"Thank you. I'll tell your manager you've helped me. Good evening." I attempt a smile, but he ignores it and leaves with a pointed, "Good afternoon."

Maybe I've lost him his job.

Or maybe everybody down in Room Service spends their days filling water bottles from the tap, from stagnant pools, from beggars' wounds, how should I know. We've made them suffer, why not? I probably earn his year's salary in a week.

I don't care, though. Not one of them is my direct responsibility.

The new seals are OK, the first one giving with a reassuring snap and letting me, finally, drink. It tastes faintly chalky and lukewarm. I run a few drops into the hollow of my palm and wipe my face.

Next year I'm taking my break in Europe, in Britain: at least then I'll be poisoned close to home. Tim never goes far: a long weekend in Antrim, the Lake District, a few days in Argyll, the Orkney Isles. He always comes back happy.

Because he's been away from me.

But if he's happy, that's when he'll do a wrong thing.

I keep drinking, probably too much.

Lips against lips while I stroke his hair, feel when he breathes, swallow when he swallows. Clever mouth, it always deepens the parting, opens it, smoothes the smooth. And then he looks up, lifts his head: Tim, sheepish and excited, at the edge of smiling. It used to be the little glance that made sure I was happy and he was allowed. Now it lets me know that this is wicked and nice because we are two strangers.

When the telephone rings, I rush a mouthful, cough.

No one but Tim knows I'm here.

"Hello?"

"Good evening. This is a single occupancy room?" It is a hotel voice, a stranger. "It is a single occupancy?"

"It's *what?*" I am conscious of the liquid weight I've loaded in.

"It is a single occupancy, what you have paid for."

"Yes. Single. Yes."

I don't want to deal with this now—whatever this is.

"You don't let our personnel clean your room. You have been there for the complete day, not leaving. Now you have two bottles of water. But this is a single occupancy room."

"Look, what are you . . . ? I've been ill. Ill."

Room Service—they're paying me back.

"I need a lot of water." There is a sceptical pause. "You can come and search if you like." And another. "Two bottles does not imply two people. I mean, if I was in the same bed with someone, we could surely share the same bloody bottle."

This is obviously a deeply improper suggestion. "I have to ask if you are alone, this is all. This is my job."

"Great, you've done your job. *Good evening.*"

I hang up, before they can say anything else.

And fuck you. Single occupancy. What else.

Then a twist of nausea shakes me, doubles me forward. Arms, legs, everything is slippy, jerking with each lunge, and I don't think I can walk and I am right, but I tumble and stagger into the bathroom, the cooler air, the business of being freed from this.

It takes a while.

And then something has altered. The stillness is more definitive. My lips seem tender, I am light-headed, but I know I won't have to be sick again.

Found the trigger, didn't I.

Some thoughts are best left quiet and I shut myself against them every day. It isn't often that they have a use.

But today they were what I needed.

A Wrong Thing

So I unlocked the morning when I smelt it on his hands and chose to ignore it, believed I was wrong, until it was there again one night, there on his face, his mouth, his lips: the scent of a stranger, of some other woman, some cunt. Tim, he noticed when I flinched, and took care to kiss me again, as if he wanted me to be quite sure that he'd done a wrong thing.

And I was sure enough to picture it, the way he would look up, happily caught in the act, before he tongued back in.

And I knew that he wouldn't leave me and that I couldn't leave him.

I still know it, the way that I know my name: Christian, Middle, Married. Now that we're strangers, we need each other's company. This won't change. And, more than any infidelity, it sickens me. It sickens me.

I wash my face with bottled water and I stand. The room is itself and I am me. Nothing has changed.

A Little like Light

You should tell everyone nothing: especially nothing about love.

Otherwise, over and over, there always will be someone who always has to ask about you, about love, about your love, and you'll end up like me—always having to answer.

By now, I know how to, of course, that isn't the problem. I shrug, I wag my hands—sometimes the one hand only—I shake my head, or I offer that little manoeuvre involving an upward jerk of my chin combined with very mildly rolling eyes. That one gets a laugh, during which I will probably smile, indulgent, and I will not ever say

I'm a sick man—you shouldn't be laughing. I am very seriously ill. I think I have diabetes—I must have diabetes. My current doctor, like all of the others, disagrees with me, but I know—I can assure you that I do have undoubted diabetes, and also leukaemia, and this thing which is removing the bone mass from my legs—perhaps elsewhere, too—it is daily reaming out a new fragility in my pelvis, an increasing insecurity when I walk, and a fear that I'll crumble something if I roll over while I'm asleep. I don't care what anyone tells me, I am deeply unwell, I couldn't ever feel this way if I were fit. And you are there and laughing and I am here and scared that I will nocturnally fragment and, set beside all this, my impotence should seem a really, wholly minor matter, but in fact it doesn't. In fact it does not. And every part of this is no one else's business, only my own, just like my love.

I married young: twenty-four: and I have stayed that way ever since. Now I am forty-three. Ten years in, and with the necessary parts still working, I fathered my son. He is called Malcolm John and I am called John Edward and, in this way, the names of our respective fathers have slipped back a notch to settle in subsidiary roles for, most likely, the duration of two other lives.

Actually, I did once think of dropping my John and enjoying the fresh sensation of being Ted. My father was steadfastly an Edward, so there would have been no confusion. I don't know why I didn't do it: a kind of stage fright, I suppose, an unwillingness to fail all over again in another role.

Malcolm, my boy Mal, I would imagine harbours no such fantasies—he thinks that I don't like him. Which is true, I don't. He is, I'm afraid, rather difficult to like. Temperamentally, he's pleasant enough: not that bright, but not so stupid, equipped with acquaintances: there is simply something about him which I find physically disturbing. He isn't exactly clumsy, he just looks as if he will be, he isn't exactly dirty, he just appears unwashed, his clothes aren't exactly rumpled, he just has a dishevelled stance. He is a mess, fundamentally. When he was still a baby with the usual murmurs of down on a warm, endearing skin, beguilingly taut with life and little veins, he was also, somehow, cloying to the touch, consistently *tacky*. Some children are born athletes, or predisposed to be good at maths. Malcolm was made to be slightly unfortunate.

Because of this, we spend a great deal of time together. We bicycle round the playing fields at weekends, we visit the cinema, I have taught him to catch, to whistle and, after a fashion, to swim. But then he will look at me, halt me with a glance from among the trees next to the long jump, or breathlessly red-eyed and glistening in the pool, and I will stop pretending and we will both remember: we aren't having fun. Any treat in each other's company is no treat at all: we are not enough. We are the only real friends that we have and, as a pair, we are a continual, mutual disappointment, frequently prey to these sad, small pauses for thought. After which we hug and hold hands for a while, because we truly are sorry for each other, but sharing sympathy is not the same as love. Then we begin again with what we have to: being a father and a son.

I think, aside from anything else, that Mal didn't get enough daylight, early on. Our house, the only one he's ever known, is snibbed between the highest part of the wall around the school and the tallest, easterly edge of what our current Head likes to call its façade. Direct light will sneak a way down through a handful of our windows for maybe three hours on a clear summer's day, which is enough to keep my window boxes going, but must fall short of what's needed for a boy. We have no garden and most of his early outdoor playing had to be done in the evenings when the classes were over and their children gone. He still looks his best in late slants of shadow, the silently incendiary glow that closes down the day.

And the buildings are set in gravel, that's another drawback—generations of youngsters have left this place with tiny granite fragments irretrievably embedded in their palms and knees. My son is just the same, little patches of him shimmering with iodine painted across fresh scabs. Now that I'm worried the necks of my femurs may snap with no warning and send me tumbling, we spend as much time as we're able out at the sports fields. We feel calmer when we can anticipate soft landings against grass.

My health also troubles me less when I'm working, although

work involves a good deal of striding about. But, on duty, I have the uniform: the shiny shoes, the bunches of keys, the peaked cap and piercing expression: the usual, invulnerable ensemble for the security guard, the prison warder—or for the janitor. I can't imagine ever having an accident while I'm dressed like this, it would offend against natural justice.

In fact, there has only been a single mishap in more than two decades of service: the massive one which continues to puzzle me. I watch my wife, peek at her when she's busy, or reading a magazine, or asleep, and I think: *This is the sort of woman who would marry a janitor.*

She has married a janitor. But I am the sort of man who has never felt like a janitor. I am the wrong man for the job. I have simply continued to be a janitor by default while I have waited to discover what I'm really supposed to do. I am an acting janitor—yes, one of many years' standing, but, all the same—this surely must make me an acting husband, too.

She bought us matching anoraks in the last January sales. They are perfectly pleasant and warm and were once expensive, but they are still matching and still anoraks—blue with blocks of purple at the shoulders and unnecessary woven tabs attached to the zips: a 44 chest for me and a 40 for her. She used to be smaller, smaller everywhere. And out we go, of a Saturday, to shop—the janitor and his better half in their matching anoraks. That can't be right.

I mean, I don't exactly mind my having to play out the janitor's part. Around the house, I tend my paintwork and window boxes the way a country stationmaster might. I guessed this was the right thing to do and it has, indeed, impressed three successive heads. My bulbs and geraniums flourish and I rarely have to dig out cigarette stubs from amongst them because, out in the school's world, I keep my population terrified. Among four- to twelve-year-olds—that's the limit to what we take—I am an undisputed king. In the boys' toilets, the only graffiti I won't have removed is a narrow line in smudgy biro that warns of the dangers of me. I didn't put it there myself.

So I don't hate the role, not entirely, it's only that acting the janitor has come to be almost all there is of me. I do object to that: my unwelcome self, the finish to my shift when I swing quickly home—it's not exactly far away—and I prise off the Doc Martens and, soft- and hot-footed, I pad straight into the type of domestic bliss designed to please a janitor, the janitor I am not. Sticky boy, dark house, a wife whose sweat, when fresh, smells large but herbal, something like the after-aroma left by crushed leaves of mint, which is weird, though also cheering and familiar—only not for me. Cheering and familiar, that isn't love.

I used to fuck her while I wore the uniform. That worked for a number of years—once a month, or so. It meant that I could combine the more comfortable side of my duties with the areas that were escalating, developing alarming filaments and structures, like a dry rot spreading up inside my future. She liked it, I think: the costume sex. My buttons were the great thing— the tiny nips of chill from them as she pulled my jacket hard against her skin and the way they'd wink in the gloom of the kitchen, or the gloom of wherever else in the house she'd caught me. Doing it this way suggested types of strange authority. We both enjoyed that.

We differed about my trousers, though. I preferred them at half-mast, this nourishing the longest-running sexual fantasy I've ever had: the one where I'm unmasked suddenly by an admiring, anonymous throng while the pale force of my arse keeps slamming manfully into the space provided between a pair of cocked and shaking legs. I do look at my best from the back—not a bit like an invalid.

My wife wanted me to march up and perform the necessary introduction with just my flies undone, giving her the full experience of the dark blue serge, so to speak. But this felt as if I was trying to screw her from inside a pillar box and, almost immediately, my zip would cramp in and saw at the base of my cock— sometimes in stereo—and then, when I'd managed everything anyway, I would tend to be left with stains to sponge off before I could go back out and face the children.

After several discussions, my wife and I, we did the married thing and compromised, took it approximately in turns to be more or less dissatisfied. And Mal's arrival put an end to our dilemma, in any case. Although I tried to keep my hat on in bed for a time, even after that. I wanted to show willing.

But while I was still performing as the fancy-dress violator, there were some afternoons and evenings, as I marched out patrolling the school, when I would realise that I still smelt of fucking. Nothing obscene, or offensive—more a slight heat in the air when I leaned forward, a vaguely electrical taste under the breath.

This, I am absolutely sure, is what made the cleaners take to me. The two younger guys I was technically in charge of would find themselves teased and harassed, almost daily, but our ladies were purely solicitous with me, as if the slight atmosphere of aftermath I sometimes brought along made them think that I must be tired, or worth spoiling. I was made cups of tea, given baking, loaned a read at their papers and magazines. In return, I'd let a few of them sit in my bothy, have a comfortable cigarette in their break.

Jean wasn't one of the smokers, but she'd wander by, too. Lovely woman, Jean, a truly decent person. When everyone first heard the terms of the private tender: the terrible money, the stupid hours: she cried solidly, right through, until it was time for them to head off home. I had to let her have my armchair and close the door. Terrible.

Now she cleans about as badly as everyone else, but there are evenings when she'll forget herself and suddenly a corridor floor will be perfect—not with a thin, shiny pathway rubbed out between the muck—clean from wall to wall, the old way. Or the taps will end up sparkling, sinks glossed, or a classroom will seem warm and tended, as if somebody cared. I gave her a box of chocolates the Christmas after our change of contracts and she blushed. So now I do it every year. This isn't so much because of the blushes, but because she may well be as out of place in her life as I am in mine. Displaced persons should know one another and be kind. If you can't have love, you can sometimes have kindness.

Once I almost told her what happened—why I'm this man and not myself. But people often think the story's funny when I don't want them to, so instead I went back and told everything to Malcolm. It's not what I'd intended, but we were stuck in one of our silences and this filled a gap.

I was hit by a cyclist. Not one on a motorbike—a cyclist: the tinny bell and pump and pedal type of cyclist. Which is ridiculous, I can see. I've been alive, as I've said, for forty-three years and I've never met anyone else who was hit by a bicycle in broad daylight: they're not tricky to spot, it isn't enormously difficult to step out of their way, they are—as far as everyone else is concerned—quite harmless. Me, I was caught full on by one and hospitalised. I was given a crack in my skull, a dislocated shoulder and a few other odds and ends which were less important, but the whole thing took up my time when I should have been studying for my first set of proper exams.

In the end I took re-sits. I didn't do well and then I couldn't settle and then, without further reason, I no longer wanted to try. My mother—who cleaned in a hospital, not a school—she'd intended me for great things and my father and I—not wage-earners—had believed her. We had enjoyed believing. But, after the bicycle hurt me, I couldn't find my pleasant expectations any more. I waited, sullen, at the back of my various classes and passed the time until each reached its end by making an echo come inside my head. Whatever jolt I'd taken to the brain had left me with the knack of modifying everything I heard—I could still do it up until my twenties. If I concentrated, sounds would waver, pause and then tip into a tumbled repetition, as if they were bouncing off my own private cliff and, every time this started up, my solitary—also echoing—thought would be: *My talent, my only one, it had to be this—the magical ability to turn any noise into something you might hear from inside a Hammond organ.* I may not have called it a Hammond organ by name, but that's what I meant.

So I left school with just enough qualifications to be a janitor: first a junior and then a senior janitor. When I told this to Malcolm, I finished with *Wasn't that handy?—I get to wear a hat* not adding *in which I used to screw your ma, when I could still manage—your mother, the first girl I met who said that she'd marry me—I was quite sure there would not be another so I didn't look.*

And, by the way, my accident is the reason why I am not a physicist, or a diver, or a great, theatrical illusionist: why I am this way and you are like that. And why did the cycle hit me in the first place? Because I was mooning about at the foot of a hill, imagining—can you believe it—the hundreds of things I might do once I was a graduate from a university. An honours degree at Oxford, St. Andrews, or Aberdeen, I had it planned out in detail. Then down came the irony and the bike.

Malcolm asked me if the cyclist was all right. He has a generous nature, Mal. I told him the man wore a helmet, so he was fine. *That's why we wear our helmets—they keep us safe.* Perhaps I should wear mine in bed.

Not that I cycle as much now as I used to, because of my diseases.

After the story, it was time that Mal turned in. Once he'd got settled, I strolled up and wished him good-night, then sat at the top of the stairs as the evening gradually tilted away towards bedtime for me and my wife. Which is not so good. My marital inabilities have become a source of tension. She has told me to see the doctor, sometimes she shouts, or I do, but for the most part we take care to separate our arrivals beneath the covers with a decent interval and then to plunge rapidly into feigned or genuine sleep.

I pressed my spine against the edge of the highest step and focused on the stairwell, pictured it as the black of a deep pool. It's soothing to think of water, gathered up in a soft column that could be private and hold me, the impression of warm rocks around it and sun and living, undutiful air.

When I first saw Elizabeth, I was doing much the same. My arms were hanging over the banisters, an easy weight, and I was staring, without minding, down from the third floor to the ground and the infants' classrooms. Then she was there.

And it shouldn't be possible to have that much attention simply scooped up out of you by the curve of someone's shoulders, the top of her head, the tone of her footfalls, the March sun through a dirty, south-facing window just slowing across the shape and the sheen of her hair. By the time she'd climbed enough to show me her face, I'd been inhaling for more than a minute. She smiled at me the way pleasant people will if they pass an inoffensive stranger. Packed with breath, I tried to lever my body away from the handrail, but I was locked there, lungs stinging. She walked softly behind me and went on through the fire door and into the top passageway. I couldn't even turn my head.

The light in the stairwell streamed with sheets and flour-ishes of dust.

I breathed out.

Elizabeth Harrison, permanent replacement teacher for Primary 5b, the most fortunate class in creation. Her predecessor, the manic Mrs. Winters, had slithered from two sick days in the week up to three and then had disappeared entirely. This makes her directly responsible for allowing me to be dumbfounded one spring morning by Elizabeth Harrison who is, in her turn, completely to blame for keeping me that way.

For the rest of the day I couldn't stop it, the dumbfounded-ness, the silly, hot pounces of intention—

If I look in her room once she's gone then I'll find . . .

*Well, what **would** I find?*

In the end, something. The room, anyway, will smell of her—her room, it stands to reason, it stands perfectly. I could bring her letters from the office in the mornings, check the windows, see how she feels she's fitting in. Tell her she should drink bottled water, the stuff here is terrible: bad pipes, I've reported and reported it.

No. I will not look in her room. Her room is in a building twelve yards away from the home of my wife and son. Which is my home also.

But I don't want it.

But I won't look in her room.

I will show her magic. I will be a magician for her, I will give her that instead.

Prestidigitation: it's another interest I don't share with my family. Useful in school, though. Our present Head doesn't approve, but in the past I have put on shows for the older classes: entertaining and good for the myth of my professional omnipotence. I taught myself; most of the things I know, I've learned about with no help but my own.

Now, in rainy lunch hours, I sometimes let a few kids into the bothy—a second janitor there to chaperon, of course, you can't be too cautious—and I give them tiny, necessary lessons in impossibility. A card can't be in my right hand and, at the same time, in my left: it can't move from somewhere to nowhere and back again: it can't be its own self and also something else. But, then again, it can, if you understand the trick of it.

At the very least, none of my pupils will be taken in by a shell game, or anything like it, and they won't bet on finding the lady: she can't be found. Some of the brighter ones may remember that nice confusion when I've pulled out fifty-pences from inside their ears, or failed to cut off their thumbs with my guillotine. When they realise, much later, that their needs deny physical laws, or that all adults are helplessly, regularly tricked and must frequently be themselves and also total strangers, then I hope they may feel they have been, in some minor way, prepared.

For Elizabeth, I laid on a private show. My hands stumbled and bumped when I opened the door for her, pointed out the best of my chairs, but they settled once I'd started the routine. I drew solid rings in and out of bottles they couldn't fit, poured pints into quarts and vice versa, took her wristwatch—with her temperature—wrapped it in a handkerchief, destroyed it with a hammer and then gave it back unharmed. She was nervous about the guillotine, so I only used it on myself. The one thing she asked to see again was the old, flip-flop roll of a coin across my knuckles, left to right and right to left, ad infinitum.

"This isn't a trick, though."

"No. I can see that."

"It's a training thing—to keep your fingers supple." This, because of the mood I was in, sounded personal and inappropriate. I kept on talking, so that I wouldn't blush. "The old magicians, they trained to incredible levels. Houdini taught himself to pick up pins using just his eyelashes."

She frowned very gently, shivered the substance of everything, "Why?"

"Because he thought he should be able to."

That, I intended to sound personal and inappropriate.

The following morning, I started to grow a moustache. I wanted to be different for her. Mal said he liked it and my wife said she did not, as if it could interfere with kisses we no longer exchanged. And, Friday afternoon, six weeks after Elizabeth Harrison had arrived, the playground all raw with the scent of spring, no kids, door closed, I leaned along her desk in her classroom and kissed her, Elizabeth.

And this is it now, isn't it? Love.

The moustache didn't interfere.

She'd been telling me about her father. We did this a lot: exchanging information, as if we were forms we'd each have to complete, would enjoy completing. There was no rush, her husband didn't collect her on a Friday, so I'd talked about these two guinea pigs I'd had when I was seven, or eight, and then we moved on to cats, her cat, the way they interrupt you on the telephone, like children—she has no children—and then her father and the way he shouts whenever he rings, as if he had to compensate for the distance set between them, and then she paused and couldn't meet my eyes and then I kissed her. On her mouth.

After that I looked to see if she needed more white chalk and I mentioned something about littering in the playground and every sound outside was somebody coming to fetch me, to make me stop, but no one arrived and I licked my lips—*she tastes of me, like me*—and she walked, came to stand at my side, and watch the evening start up through the windows.

"Why did they put down gravel, do you think?"

"Because they don't like children." My voice seeming very small, or my self grown larger and hot. "Schools never really do."

"That's a terrible thing to say."

And the room rolled to make me face her, hold her for balance, and again kiss. Elizabeth's hands caught behind me, low, at the small of my back, precisely where a heavy, silvery feeling had started to flower and seep, as soon as we closed ourselves in that first touch.

"I'm glad I have this classroom." Her voice on my neck, sleek under my shirt, inside my ribs: the key to open me. "It gets so much sun."

Trying not to twitch against her, flinch, wanting to be only smooth, secure. "You might not be so glad in the summer."

"I can keep the windows open."

"Yes. You can do that."

When we swayed apart, she brushed the hair above my ear, which made me feel sick: in a good way, sick. I couldn't think of anything to do back. "Well, I'll see you on Monday, then." Which I hadn't meant to sound as if I'd be leaving, but then again, I didn't know how to stay. My pulse had thickened, it was making everything jump, I was sure it would be visible.

And is that what she'd like to see? I mean, are we both being care-
ful, or is it that we're not meant to care when we happen to each other
and taste like each other—are we not supposed to say? We do this as if
we're not doing this? Does she know that I'm hard now? Does she
want that or not? Me or not?

I walked to the door and was, the whole time, dropping into the dark of a pool, something that muffled my breath.

Here I am, though, myself. This is me now, found. This is love.

Schools are watchful places, full of little eyes, but Elizabeth and I, we were invisible, truly. I adored it: to pass across the playground and glance up, find the shape of her, looking down, class out of sight. We would never acknowledge each other, but we would know. Just as we did in the crowd at assembly when I might pass her without a sign, then lean by the doorway, unsteadied as the thought of her rose in me, detonated: so much beauty.

So much beauty. And we do know, don't we? We do both know.

In the end, I told Mal. I didn't want to, but I needed to make my love exist out loud.

At this time, he was five, I think, or just six, and before he slept we'd talk, or I'd read to him, make up stories. *In a desert, in a castle, in a dungeon, there was a prison guard and everyone thought he was nobody special and he agreed.* The guard, he was our favourite—close enough to me to be familiar, far enough away for us to like him. He was called Ted and he fought with the usual monsters, some of them from outer space, but then headed for home to be in love with his lady. She looked, in each story, not unlike Malcolm's mother, because I'm not a fool. *But his love for her was new every time he met her, it made him better than himself, it was like being hungry and on holiday and wanting Christmas and feeling that it's close.*

Well, how do you describe your love to anyone, let alone a child—and please let us not quite mention that all of this need for Elizabeth removed any erection that I might have still kept for my wife. Nothing doing there for her now, not a thing. *Love is like the best surprise you can think of every morning, licking right over your skin.* Which probably means that Malcolm thinks love tickles—although that wouldn't really disturb me, as long as he knows it's supposed to be good.

And it is. My face in her hair, yes: being there for the heat, the intention, that lights her face, our hands making every clasp and slip I can imagine, every one, and the first time she opened the seal of her mouth, yes, and easing and setting and pressing my body against hers and trying to think away our clothes, yes—this is mine with Elizabeth, but there is nothing more. We only have love, we don't make it.

So I can't fuck my wife—domestic impotence—and, with Elizabeth, although I'd be very much able and want to and need to and could at a moment's notice, or possibly less, it never does happen, not quite. In accordance with my wishes and against them—either way, I just no longer fuck.

This hurts me, if I think of it. And I think of it a lot.

Once, for two whole free periods we sat together in the boiler room. Elizabeth's class were at the swimming baths without her—drowning in the care of others, for all that it mattered to me. That gave us an hour and a half in powdery, dimmed light, warmth flexing in the pipes around us, and nothing to do but talk about ourselves and what we liked.

There was more to do than that—it was perfectly clear there was more—but we didn't do it. Tugged her in at the side door, I'm not even certain she knew it was there, but she didn't complain—stepped right down and came with me, holding my hand. And then facing each other, whispering, we traded our details, the places, the ways: her first—and once in a park with her boyfriend when she was twenty—the crowd I always dream will catch me—my first—and that, every time, I want to stay inside, even after, to be inside, feel everything.

"So you're demanding."

"No." The air was felty, dry, it kept making me cough. "I'm not. I'm very easily satisfied, but what I like, I like very much."

I'd hoped that she might say the same thing back, or something similar, but she didn't and you would suppose, wouldn't you, that you'd describe these things to each other as a couple, because you intended to both make each other comfortable, happy, fucked. Your conversation would not be entirely purposeless.

That is what you might reasonably suppose.

I ended the afternoon unable to move. She kissed the top of my head—the only time we touched that day—and then she rushed the stairs to be ready for her lift. I stared at the pipes, the storage boxes—full of old sheet music for some reason—and I read the instructions on the fire blanket, over and over again. Something was going wrong in my bones, I realised that, and it seemed I was ill in a number of ways now, or would be soon. My scalp ached where her lips had rested on my hair.

Did you know, the man who invented the in-car cigarette lighter, the one with the little element you plug into the dash, he was a magician. He'd needed to set things burning, unseen, and that was his solution to the problem: very neat. The way I've heard the story, a big car company took the idea and the magician never got a penny for it and no credit either. Stuck in the basement until my legs could bear my weight, I thought about that.

Do all the work and then you get nothing, not a sign of fucking hope. Anticipation with no future, you know what that is—a definition of despair.

And I had long enough there to consider that, if she didn't love her husband and she had started this love with me but wouldn't finish, then perhaps I had opened a door for her and somebody else entirely had used it to slip in.

Do all the work and you get nothing.

I made it across to one of the boxes, crawling, and threw up on multiple copies of "I'd Like to Teach the World to Sing."

Poor Malcolm, he didn't get to sleep at his proper time for quite a few nights after that, although I wasn't keeping him up with stories: I hadn't the heart for Ted, much less for his lady, or his love. I kept to facts. Mal never does seem to be lonely, but I hope that knowing practical information may help him when he's with the other boys. I've let him use a soldering iron—with predictably lumpy results—he can rewire a plug and understands pulleys and gears. I do want to help my son. So, for example, I sat on his bed for those evenings after the boiler-room incident and told him why stars twinkle and why a fire engine's siren changes as it passes and what is inertia. I tried to do the right, the paternal thing, even though I was glad in the deep dark of my heart that Malcolm was so isolated: the frightening janitor's son: and that this meant the shouting matches and screamed comments about my prick were caught firmly inside my house with my family and, equally, any minor mentions of Elizabeth out in the world were kept at bay and I was safe—safe to do very little, but even so.

Malcolm, remember when we drove last summer? On the road there was water you could see, but never reach, because it wasn't really there. It seemed to be magic, but it was only the way the world works.

Sometimes I didn't know if he understood me—he would look puzzled, or else tired, and it was hard to tell between them.

Light—I've told you about light, the way it comes in little pieces and also in long lines, both at the same time and never mind if that's impossible. Well, light always knows the quickest way to go. It's slower through water and cold air, so it avoids them. When we drive, if we're up in cold air and so is the sun, but down on the road there's some warm air in a dip, then the sun's light will pick out the quickest path to our eyes, ducking down through the warm air and then up again. So we see sky light, coming from the ground and it looks like water, reflecting the sun, although there isn't any water there at all. The light always knows what to do, like magic.

This was the point where I started praying: nothing very formal, just requests for help. I am not religious, never have been, my father was a communist, but thinking hadn't helped me and nor had planning, wishing, avoiding her, seeking her out. On a Saturday afternoon, my wife caught me—at prayer. I had to pretend I was looking for something I'd dropped under the bed. Don't ask me why I'd used the bedroom in the first place— Christopher Robin with his elbows on the quilt, or the place I associated most with a need for divine intervention, nothing was clear to me any more—but that was where I'd ended up. I glanced round and my wife was standing, quiet, behind me, I felt as if she'd trapped me stealing from her, or having a wank, and she gave me a look as if she wished she had. I only spoke to God in the bathroom after that.

And prayers get answered, they do. My sole, repetitive effort certainly got a reply.

"I'm going."

She mentioned a primary school on the north side of our town while my breathing stiffened to a halt and then panicked back in, too fast.

"Bill's already there."

Bill, her husband, was a teacher, too. I'd watched him from a distance—he dressed badly and you'd have sworn that his mother still cut his hair. "Well, is that good? Do you want to be . . ." I was going to finish with *both in the same school,* in a voice which suggested it would give rise to tensions and many other kinds of hell. But we already knew about that, so I didn't bother. I sat on the lip of her desk, afraid. "Oh." I couldn't remember being so wholly afraid.

"Once I'm settled, I'll call."

When we kissed I drew her tongue hard into my mouth, hoped it hurt a little, let my hands slide to her arse and hold her as I hadn't often attempted to, for fear of getting nowhere and then going insane.

I am a janitor, I am not a man that women call. No one, ever in my life, has called me, not that way.

I went insane, in any case. Nothing spectacular: I think I was the only one who knew. They were supposed to have a leaving do in school to send Elizabeth off in style, and I was meant to go along and contribute a few tricks. But I wasn't well that week and I think, even before, they'd changed their minds and settled for a pub night out.

On the Monday morning, people talked about their hangovers and said they'd had fun, and walking across the playground was something I avoided for a while, because there was no more Elizabeth Harrison. I tried not to hate the supply who turned up to replace her. Supplies these days, they know nothing, they're what we get instead of teachers.

I kept praying for about a week, but it seemed to bring on no additional effects. Mrs. Campbell, who deals with the dim half of Primary One, is mad enough to consult the *I Ching* before she makes any decision and is also mad enough to say so. I borrowed her copy, bided my time, and then sneaked with it upstairs, bolted the door, and threw out the little sticks provided to make their pattern on the toilet lid—this not only guaranteed my privacy, I thought, but seemed completely appropriate.

He cannot help whom he follows and is dissatisfied in his mind. The situation is perilous and the heart glows with suppressed excitement.

Those were the only bits that made sense. Except that it did also highlight the bones in my legs that now seemed to feel thinner, raw. It closed with *there will be good fortune* but then I supposed that most predictions would end that way, just to keep you consulting. I wanted to believe it, though: knew that I shouldn't, because good fortune doesn't happen to a man like me.

"John?" She'd phoned my number in the bothy, had to call three or four times, "Hello? Is that you?" until she found me in and, as it happened, alone. "John, it's Elizabeth."

As if I hadn't known.

"Yes, yes, I . . . Hello." That soft pool was yawning for me and I jumped, sprang at it like a happy suicide. "Are you, ahm . . . are you well?"

"Yes. You?"

I couldn't find an answer. Elizabeth didn't wait for one, she only had a minute before she needed to get back, but she wanted to see me, Thursday night, the bar of a hotel I'd never heard of, away on the edge of town.

A hotel.

That week I steered Malcolm and Ted through a barrage of trials and monsters, but I kept them away from the castle. *A hotel.* If Ted had got near to his lady, I couldn't have been responsible.

A hotel.

My wife got a different story—that I'd run out of good window mastic, but Steve over at St. Saviour's said he'd got some, I'd go over and pick it up, have a drink. Steve enjoys a drink and decent mastic is, occasionally, hard to find. I would have believed me.

And I stepped out on Thursday in nondescript trousers but, underneath that terrible anorak, I wore the good jacket, my nicest shirt—I don't really have many that aren't white—and the best tie. In one of my tiny, stupid, zippered pockets, I had two condoms for no reason.

Not to use, I don't think I'll use them, not one of them. But if I did need them and I hadn't got them, Jesus.

I ought to have known. Primary One's *I Ching* said: *The situation is perilous. No movement in any direction should be made.* And she is Elizabeth and I am this man and not another and so I should have understood what I could expect.

That she would smell fresh from a bath: those different little perfumes: the quiet, clean evening taste of a woman whenever you breathe in, swallow: and the scent of her skin: her reachable skin that you kiss on her cheek and near her lips, brush with your hand—slowly, seriously, the way it should be done, finding your lady. And you want to see her tonight completely, everything, to break her sweat against you, to howl and race and shiver until you are happy, both of you.

But when we meet, it doesn't make us happy, it just makes us want to be.

I realised, as soon as I saw her face, that she hadn't booked a room, that we would stare at our dinners together in the broad, mainly sand-coloured restaurant and that I would drink slightly too much and then would take coffee—I know it seems unlikely, but I think six coffees—to make the meal last.

If anyone had seen us, the way we were, we'd have been in just as much trouble as if we had gone upstairs together, as if we'd fucked across the table while the waiter brought over our eleventh and twelfth complimentary-with-coffee mints.

We stood in the foyer for too long before we left, the porter was edging looks at us, anticipating the final agreement, the turn, the mumbled request for a double room. He didn't know what we're like. Our hands patted and dabbed at shoulders, forearms, and nothing connected properly. Quietly we wished each other the good night we weren't going to have and walked out to separate cars in the dark. I shouldn't have been driving, but then there are lots of things I shouldn't do and I wouldn't be myself without them.

This is love. This terrible feeling. This knowing I would rather see her than be content. Even the way that we are is so near to being enough. This is love.

This is love as I understand it. I could be wrong. I would rather not talk about it, I do imagine that would be best. Malcolm, though, whenever I think he's moved on, he'll sit up in bed and want to hear about it. In the end, he always has to ask. Perhaps he realises that I probably need him to, that without him I would come back from February's restaurant, April's cinema, May's hotel: from each of my unconcluded meetings with Elizabeth: and I wouldn't know what to do.

Although it won't ever be anything other than inappropriate, I would like to tell him, to really say:

A Little like Light

The best love is a little like light. It is unremitting, cannot fail to find you, to take the shortest, surest way, as if that were marked out as part of your nature, the line where you and love are made to meet. It is your law, the physics of your life. It will move from somewhere to nowhere and back again and it will make you lost. It is beautiful and terrible and blinding and you will never understand the trick of it.

For Shelby White and Leon Levy

How to Find Your Way in Woods

The thunder had battered and turned above the house for most of the night and they had stayed in their separate bedrooms, Sarah watching the woods cracked open, stripped out of the dark. The grass, the trees, the bushes, everything was trapped for uneasy seconds beneath a sudden, lilac sky and then the window glass would shrug back into secrecy and show no more than her reflection, shivered in the roar of aftershocks and pale.

That bleached face in the pane had surprised her, the narrowness of its mouth, an almost untrustworthy shift in the eyes as they'd looked beyond her and to the charged edge of the clearing. She had seemed to be slightly older than she was and, literally, more shallow: someone who really, in some way, had not lived a good life. There was nothing definitely evil or unpleasant there, just a sense of being insubstantial, second rate. This had only been to do with the light, the strangeness of the light, but still she felt uncomfortable in the morning, as if she'd misplaced a belonging she was fond of.

"God, it was terrific. I nearly went outside." Twenty past nine and David was leaning in the kitchen doorway. He looked tired, as she supposed she must, but he seemed contented, too, relaxed. "Did it wake you?" For the first time, she imagined that he might be glad he'd come.

"Of course it woke me."

When David passed her, she noticed he smelt of himself and of the privacy of sleep. He sat at the table and stretched, easy. "You weren't frightened?"

He hadn't shaved yet. She wasn't used to seeing him with bristles, or in a dressing gown, for that matter. Sarah liked to wait until her first few coffees had kicked in before she changed out of her night things. She hadn't seen a reason to behave any differently just because David was here, but for his part he'd been careful, on each of their previous days, to appear only once he was fully groomed and dressed. However he'd intended she should feel about this, it had struck her as defensive, a tiny but unmistakable rebuff with each breakfast they shared.

"Well, were you . . . ? Frightened?"

"Did you think I would be?" It wasn't as if she couldn't be trusted not to leap on him.

"You don't get that kind of storm in Britain." His voice was lower this early, had a delicacy to it that was new.

At least she thought it was new. "But we get them all the time over here." And he wasn't that attractive, she'd have said. Not any more. "Some use you'd have been, if I *was* scared."

"I'm good at making people not scared." He said this lightly, but still made her remember that she didn't especially know him now, that more than enough time had passed to leave them distant.

"Well, I'd have to take your word for that." She hadn't fully intended to sound sour, but knew she had, in any case, and so she made an effort to smile next. "I could have been paralysed with horror. You didn't rush through to check. You didn't even saunter through to check . . ."

David widened his eyes for an instant and then took her glance, drew it, and lit a live pause in her before he blinked away. He'd always used to do that, make the look—*we are together, whatever we say.* Her smile receded, unsure of itself. In bars, at parties, when they were having Sunday dinner with his mother—wherever, really—the look had meant they'd be alone soon, part the last air between them, no more interruptions, only picking up each other's time again, touch after touch. They would kiss on their way, impatient in the crook of stairs, in corridors, the car—wherever, really.

Now it didn't mean anything, though, not today. It was a silly mistake, a nervous tic: one that turned her breath, but only by accident. Why signal he wanted to get her alone when nobody else was here?

He grinned at her and then, before she could speak, dodged in with, "You're not going to take that back?"

"Take what?"

"You're saying you genuinely needed me to check? You're sticking with that? You seriously want me to consider that you might have found the storm upsetting? You." He tapped his cup's rim. "Sarah," softly, "Guardham," marking every word. "The woman sitting in front of me." This last, as if it were something he found pleasant—Sarah facing him, the two of them together, by themselves.

Which made the words dry in her throat. "I might not be the way you remember. It's been a while . . ."

"Yes, I know. But you haven't changed. Have you?" He watched her, tried to make his smile begin another question, one he wouldn't say. "Well?"

"I'm older—"

"Are you different?"

"No." And this was no more wrong than *yes* but still she had to aim the words at the window behind him, at the damp, green, morning light. When he stayed silent, she turned to face him and saw that his eyes were closed, his head angled a little to one side. He let out a brief, thin breath, after which the line of his lips flattened and his mouth set tight.

She hadn't meant to upset him, "David?" but she'd managed to, all the same.

"It's OK. I heard. You're no different." He began to get up. "I should shave, get tidied up."

"You don't have to." Although there was no point in her speaking, because he wasn't different, either. "Not for me." If he wanted to be angry then he would be: instantly heavy with it, sealed.

"I do have to—for me." He stared at her as if she were that woman in the window, an unattractive fake.

"What if I asked you not to."

"Don't be silly." He yawned, something insincere about the movement, and then removed the pleasure from her memory of the night. "Actually, I didn't think you'd be scared of the thunder. In fact, when the whole thing began, I just jumped out of bed and I didn't even . . . Well, you know."

And she did know: he would have continued with *and I didn't even think of you* and, rather than hurt her feelings, he'd made her finish off his sentence and hurt them herself.

"Well, go and get a shave, then." Her voice abrasive and middle-aged—almost embarrassing. "You need one." She watched him leave: the small plume of hair near his crown that wouldn't lie flat, the drape of the dressing gown against him, the soft rise and fall of his bare feet. He had a stiff, short stride, something pompous about it.

Sarah decided to throw away the pan of bacon. They hadn't got around to eating it, but still this wasn't sensible: they could have the stuff cold later on, after all, it hadn't outlived its usefulness, but their argument would mean it wouldn't taste right—the way that lightning was supposed to spoil fresh milk. She didn't want it, so out it would go and, if David felt the need for bacon later, he could cook his own.

She cleared the table and washed up listening to the small, pedantic din of his preparations for the day: the drumming of a long, thorough shower, the bathroom clatter, his razor whining lightly while he stared at himself, she supposed, as he used to, with a sort of studious regret. There was a touch of temper about the louder impacts and once she heard his voice in a low punch of unintelligible complaint. He made the house cramp in against her.

So she walked out and on to the deck. The sun had risen enough to strike the planking fully and lift its moisture in a softly swinging mass of steam. Signs of the storm were everywhere, white tears and breaks in the canopy, drifts of torn leaves, the smell of drying timber and washed earth. A woodpecker trotted, picking through the grass at the clearing's edge, intent on fallen insects.

And this was what she'd wanted when she moved here, a clean place for watching nothing much happen quietly. There was a spare room, of course, but she'd never considered that anyone would use it. Come back after thirty-three years and that was what you got: no visitors. Mother in the Lutheran churchyard and father in the Episcopalian and no sense in leaving flowers now when she'd missed both funerals, along with the silences and arguments, the whole mess of it long, long gone. There were some cousins close to Norwalk, she thought, but she couldn't remember them. Anyway, she hadn't missed the people, she'd come home for the New England colours. She'd wanted to have that sea-faded look to everything again: even inland, that dusting of salt, that blue in the weather's eye.

Somewhere behind her, she heard a door slam, followed by the lighter clack of its screen and then the tump of irritable feet.

David was off for a walk, then, going somewhere without her. He could have done that in Manchester, where he belonged.

She listened to his solid progress along the narrow path beside the house. First the woodpecker started up, its wings flaring out two loops of white in the shade and then, off to the east, the crows began to barrack anxiously. The man was a complete disturbance. Next she could make out the red shout of his sweater, broken by leaves, and the pallor of his hands and face, pressing on. He'd have raised his first sweat already: the humidity wrapping in close again to muffle and punish the slightest effort. Poor old David, perpetually over-dressed.

Sarah thought she might as well take a shower herself, get on with the day as if he'd never arrived. But then she realised he'd left the path and stopped, was facing her through the trees, looking up from the clear foot of the rise. At this distance, his expression was unclear, but she could read the sad tilt to his shoulders.

And, although she didn't want to, she remembered that night near the end when they'd argued and he'd walked off, as usual, but then not gone away. Instead, he'd stood at the bar by himself with his back to her, not drinking, not speaking to the people at his side, and when she'd seen how he was, every line in him miserable, she'd wanted to go over and kiss him, stroke his neck. But he was the one who'd decided to be alone so she'd felt the soft dart of need under her ribs and had declined to answer it. She'd left the pub without him, spent the night awake in the flat, perfectly aware that, this time, he wouldn't come back.

He was here now, though, motionless and being unhappy at her all over again. This was ridiculous. She was strongly tempted to wave, but knew that David wouldn't like it—his sense of humour could fade extremely easily.

*And I've got no idea what you **would** like. I didn't ever know that. And I tried to find out, you can't say I didn't try.*

She lifted one hand to her face and touched back her hair, then folded her arms, only the rail between her and the dogged nudge of his attention.

I'd go inside now, if he wasn't still out there, being absurd.

David being David, every time the same, every time needing to have his own way. Now he was making sure that she couldn't leave without being inadvertently insulting and couldn't stay without feeling his touch, ghosted over her skin.

Although that's probably not his intention, it's just happening. Once I'm dressed, I won't feel a thing.

Then, because he'd seen whatever he'd wanted, or else decided it wouldn't be shown, he turned back for the path abruptly, almost stumbling, scrub and low branches closing behind him quickly until he was out of sight.

I never understand what he means, he just isn't clear. And, whatever else he can say about me, I am that, I was always that—I do make myself clear. What I wanted and didn't, I said everything, it wasn't my fault that he didn't believe me, that he thought I'd intended something else. He put words in my mouth, in my mind. It had nothing to do with me. And it was years ago, years, why on earth set that sort of confusion off again? Why can't he just be here and be calm? I'm calm.

Her bathroom was full of him. Not that he wasn't neat, didn't clean up nicely wherever he'd been, it was just that his presence was obvious: in the extra towel, still heavy with water, in the primly zipped spongebag, in the wet cling of the shower curtain.

But there's nothing better for tension than a good shower. She rinsed out the bath, readied the jet of water—he seemed to like it cooler than she did—and then stepped in. *I'd forgotten how it was. A couple of days with him, a couple of minutes with him when he's in a mood, and I get that scrabbling sensation above my eyes. So I end up in the shower, washing it away. By the time we'd finished, it's a wonder that I hadn't grown webbed feet.*

And maybe he was in here before, trying to wash off the worst of me. Maybe we just do this to each other.

But I'm calm. I will be calm.

She was probably standing about where he'd stood, as naked as he must have been.

Oh, and he would make a meal of that: the subtext and the convoluted thinking, so many meanings that in the end it's all meaningless.

Like the card—the inexplicable card—the one that he didn't have to send. For ten Christmasses there had been nothing, which she quite understood: she was, after all, for most of that time, quite married to somebody else.

*And that was destined to be a great success, of course. Six months after David's over with, I get married, because I've finally found something right, or near enough right, or at least **simple,** and marrying will make it last for ever and ever, amen.*

Closed the bedroom door behind us on our honeymoon night and I could barely breathe. I had to tell my blushing bridegroom that I'd got a stomach bug—anything not to face it, not that time.

Which, if I think about it, was David's fault.

She still had no idea of how or why he'd found her. But, for whatever reasons, his card had arrived last December: a moderately sized, rather sober-looking card of the Christmas variety. His handwriting hadn't improved, what there was of it, crawling above and below the usual Yuletide sentiments.

Sorry this took so long.

As if she'd been waiting for him, and then:

I do hope it is a happy Christmas,
same for the New Year.
This is my number. If you want to, call.

"If you want to." David's way of saying what he wanted and felt she should want, too.

He knew I'd be curious—and on my own. He didn't say, but he must have heard I was on my own.

"God, I'm glad." As if they'd never stopped speaking, had only taken a beat or two for breath. "Well . . . you really did, you called. And I'm in." It pleased her that she'd made him sound flustered. "God . . . Sorry. Where are you calling from? I wasn't sure of the address . . ."

"America."

"Holiday?"

"No, I went home. I live here." And a silence is only a silence, but she did remember that his seemed hurt and so she'd added, "But they're forwarding my post," only to fill up the space. "You were lucky, I think they'll stop soon. I can't remember how long I paid for." And then, when he still said nothing, "It's a service. You know . . . that you buy. I don't, in fact, get many letters from over there now. Or cards." And he'd pulled her in, staying quiet like that, almost as if there was nobody on the line, except that she could tell the difference, she'd felt him there, known her being so far away had actually upset him, could understand that from the soft irregularity of his breath. "Ah, I don't know, but— do you want to come?" She'd only said it to be friendly, "To visit?" And because she must have wanted him to, "You could?" It was odd that she hadn't known she'd ask.

"Oh, that's . . . that sounds as if it would be . . . very inconvenient."

"Inconvenient?" David hadn't lost the knack of making her feel clumsy, superfluous. "Yes, I suppose it would be. I'm a freelance, I forget other people have—"

"No, no, no. I meant inconvenient for *you*." She'd heard the slither of anxiety under his words—it was generally easier to make him anxious than it was to make him content. He'd paused and went on more cautiously, "I would, I could . . . my holidays aren't . . . the summer would be the best time. Would that be a good time?" She did want him to be content, did want to help him be that way.

"That would be a good time."

"That would be a good time?"

"Yes. A good time. Yes." And, after a strangely inadequate effort, they had both seemed to be more than content, happy.

But I didn't ask him what he meant by a good time.

And through each of the other calls and the making of arrangements, neither of them had dwelt on why she'd made the invitation, or why he'd accepted it. Sarah supposed that neither of them was willing to risk an enquiry.

Should I dress as though I care what he thinks, or to be comfortable, or what?

She let the water fall against her for a long time: it wasn't as soothing as she'd hoped.

It doesn't matter. In another four days he'll be gone.

That doesn't matter, either.

By the time David reappeared, she had slipped on the old shirt and jeans she wore to go out in the woods and was listening to the radio. A few miles upstate, the storm had brought down power lines, a tree had crushed the roof of someone's summer house, but no one, so they said, had been hurt.

"We were lucky."

David was in the kitchen, his head bent to the tap, drinking the water as it ran. "What?" He turned to her, lips and chin wet, his eyes faintly guilty. "Sorry. Should have used a glass." The heat of the walk had left his face unguarded, young—the way it had looked when she met him at the airport, when he first saw her and waved and marked her out in the crowd as someone who was meeting someone, a person who would soon be off to continue a large and friendly life. "Sorry." She'd thought then it would be all right, that he wouldn't spoil it and neither would she.

"No need to be sorry. You've saved the washing up. Did you have a good walk?"

"Mm." He drifted one hand under the tap, let it cool, then wiped it, dripping, across his forehead, his cheek, the side of his throat. "Hot, though." Moisture gathered at the corner of his eye and then descended.

"Did you see anything worth the trip?"

He bent away from her and shut the water off. "I saw a lot." Then he gave her his back, leaned against the worktop. The short trim of his hair showed up the grey. At the nape of his neck there was a rise of white.

Still, men can get away with that—looks dreadful on a woman. I can't recall when I started to use dye. He'll have seen the packet in the bathroom. Not that I care.

"See anything special?" She tried to make the question casual, as if he could take his pick of meanings and she wouldn't mind.

This time in a mumble, as if he regretted repeating it, "I saw a lot." He shifted his weight to one hip. "But I don't know what I'm looking at, half the time, maybe more than that."

She took a step in towards him, made the decision: "That's because you're in a foreign country."

"Then help me out." Something in the way he asked made the light seem different, hazardous.

She stepped in again and reached to put a hand on each of his shoulders.

"Don't do that." But he didn't move and didn't stop her.

"You asked me to help you out."

"But that doesn't help." He shrugged up his shoulder, angled his head and then let his chin rest its edge on the fingers of her left hand. "That makes me not know where I am."

"You're here."

"That doesn't help."

They stayed together without moving then, Sarah feeling the damp of his skin, the little blink of muscle when he swallowed, the flat heat of his shoulders, stiff with a resistance beyond her control, a lack of trust.

Eventually, he sighed and straightened his neck. She withdrew her hands, moist now and still slightly weighted with the echo of his shape, the negative of touch.

They'll smell of him, but I'll wash them and then they won't.

David turned and faced her. "Sorry."

"Uh hu."

"No, I mean it: I shouldn't have—"

"Neither should I."

He looked very tired now, but otherwise she couldn't tell if he was angry, happy, sad, indifferent, content. Kissing him, she was sure, would be quite inappropriate, but if he didn't leave soon, she would try it, anyway.

"Why don't you get some more sleep, David?"

"Because I'm not—" he stopped himself, lifted half a grin and shook his head. "No, you're right. I am wavery, a bit. Maybe things will be better when I've had another couple of hours."

"Are things bad at the moment?" She knew she shouldn't ask—didn't even want an answer—certainty, when it closed on her, was far more frightening than doubt.

"Are they . . . ?" He rubbed his eyes. "I'm not sure . . . I will go and sleep, though. That's a good idea." He nodded to her, his face briefly defenceless, and she needed to feel his skin again, stung with its absence.

When he woke and came through, at almost five, she cooked them both new bacon and scrambled eggs and, between them, they ate the best part of a loaf in toast.

"Oh, that's the stuff." He wiped his plate clean with a slice of cold bread in a way that suggested she might have to cook something else. "I'd forgotten we haven't eaten all day." He glanced at her briefly, enquiring. "Unless you managed something while I wasn't here."

"I didn't manage anything."

"Glad I'm indispensable." He studied the fold of bread.

"It was too hot to eat."

He breathed a small, unamused laugh, and Sarah understood that they would fight again, if she didn't manage this more sensibly.

Except, if we don't fight, then I have to—We would both—I don't know. I don't want to hurt him. I don't want to hurt me.

"David? I'd like us to do something."

"What?"

He met her eyes with a level of concern that was almost insulting, but she only looked back at him and made herself calm.

"I'd like us to go out together."

"Where?" He sounded neither pleased nor alarmed.

"Only outside, into the woods. I'd like to . . ." She could hardly say *I'd like to show you something*—she would just laugh, or he would, the thing wouldn't work, anyway. "I'd like to prove I've changed."

"In the woods."

"I've started tracking—animals, you know? I work in the evenings, mainly, putting the research together and emailing it off, so the days are my own."

"And you spend them *tracking?*" He wasn't worried any more, so he could settle into mocking: he was good at that.

"You'll see. Go and get your shoes and I'll show you." Sarah wasn't as good a tracker as she might be: she couldn't move soundlessly over dry leaves, or definitely tell an opossum's handprint from that of a young raccoon, none of that stuff.

I can still show him what I have to, though. Why not.

She watched him leave to do as she'd asked. He didn't appear to be scared, although she realised she was.

But, in the end, why not.

As they moved away from the house, the sunlight was reddening. It made them shield their eyes, laid a clean tissue of heat across their faces and pushed the shadows in long, low angles across the path. She knew they weren't walking quietly enough, but that it would be fine, because they would sit soon, when they came to the stream, and the forest would settle and get used to them.

"Hide near water and something will come to drink. You let their own need bring them to you."

"How long will we have to wait?" He was whispering, because she had.

"I don't know—until the need arises." It was good to be whispering, shoulder by shoulder, crouching just within each other's heat.

"It'll be dark soon."

"I can find the way home after sunset." That wasn't a lie— she'd done it once. But she'd had a torch then and she didn't now. "If we keep low and still, things will arrive."

"What things?"

"The deer move in the evening." White tails, they were lovely, but neither she nor David was in enough cover to let them come near. "Birds . . . I don't know. It's always different. Once a woodchuck came over those rocks: we saw each other and both froze. Woodchucks can look very like rocks, they have the right colouring, so he turned his head sideways and flattened and I'd never have guessed he was there if I hadn't known." She was talking too much when she shouldn't be talking at all, but David was listening and the woods smelt live and it was cooler here, in the shade, a good place for them both to be, so she kept on.

"Every ten minutes or so, he'd rearrange his feet, or sit up and stroke his whiskers, have a good look, and there I was, looking back. Then he'd snap into being a rock again. We went on for nearly an hour, possibly longer, with him being scared but curious and then curious but scared."

"How did you know it was a he?"

"I guessed."

"I thought things weren't supposed to know you're watching."

"Sometimes they know, but they don't mind. It's possible to be there together and no harm done."

David eased back slightly, making himself more comfortable, and gave a neutral nod. She could think of nothing else to say.

Slowly, the peace of the woods distilled into the drilling of a sap sucker, a blue jay's cry, the undulating bounce of squirrels through the scrub, the rattle of a broken branch, finally let go. She loved the clasp of it, fixing her, as one call started another and each motion found its reaction without subtext or ambivalence.

"Why did you do it?"

He made her start, although he was speaking very quietly.

"Do . . . ?"

"Why did you do it. You said you were thinking, only taking time away to think and then you were with someone else, you were *married* to someone else. Did you know him before, or . . . ? I couldn't . . ."

"I didn't know him before, he just wasn't you. We didn't work, David." Although this wasn't what she wanted to tell him, but he'd made her angry and now it was out, "I'm sorry, but—"

"*You're* sorry? I was outside the church, that's how sorry I was. I wanted to see so that I'd believe it. You got out of the car . . ." He swallowed, frowned. "I went away. But I . . . I don't know why I'm here now."

"I don't know why I asked you to be."

And it would have been good to laugh at this point and ease the atmosphere. They had, after all, just wounded themselves in faultlessly hushed tones out of consideration for animals which would, nevertheless, have heard them and kept sensibly away. Their consideration for each other was, of course, less perfect.

David tugged at a green twig, snapped it. "Look, do you mind if we don't sit out here all night. I'm getting bitten to hell by these flies and I'm not in the mood."

"Sorry to have brought you out."

"No, the idea was fine." He smiled, but not for her. "It would have been great if we'd been two other people."

"But we're not."

"What?"

"Nothing." Sarah rose and started to lead him back. "Come on. We'll at least catch the sunset."

"Oh, well, not a completely wasted day, then."

"And just when I was thinking this could only get worse if you decided you were going to be sarcastic."

"Sarah, I—"

But she grabbed his arm, pulled it, hard. "You should look at this."

"Oh for Christ's . . . now what?"

Sarah felt curiously relieved: because today had already gone so wrong that whatever she did could have no particular weight, she could simply do it anyway, because she felt like it. She kneeled and, although she didn't expect it, he also sank beside her and repeated more gently, "Now what?"

"You see where there are leaves from the last storm?"

"I suppose, yes. The dead ones."

"They bed down in a sort of layer and then they show up dips." She was proud of this, they weren't easy to spot, not from above, not walking, not in the company of a man you'd like to slap. "And then if you lift them . . ." She peeled up a section of the cover, it tore away like damp, heavy paper. "Yes. There we are." It was nice to be right, once in a while.

"Are we?"

It was a print, the split impression of a deer's hoof, sharp in the mud. "If you lean forward . . ."

"Oh, right." And it did seem that she'd pleased him, that he wanted this.

"You can go first, then."

"First at what?"

"At what I'll show you." She took his wrist, "You put," and folded all but his first two fingers into his palm, "That's right . . ." She let go. "And then you put your fingers in."

She watched as he set his fingers, one in each side of the cleft in the mud where the hoof had splayed apart.

"Lovely, isn't it? Makes you think of the moment the deer touched and left it. You'll be a bit muddy now."

"I don't mind." He paused, his concentration on his hand, and then withdrew. "Your turn."

Sarah reached and fitted into the mark while David waited. When she touched the place, she knew it at once, almost laughed.

"What's the matter?"

"It feels warm where you've been. Usually they're cold."

"Is that an improvement?"

"Yes."

The last of the sun had soaked into the leaves above them and each branch was burning with a green, veined shine.

David cleared his throat. "Shall we go home now?"

"If you want to."

They stood, unsteady for an instant.

"David?"

"Yes."

"I thought we were over. When I tried to go back and you—"

"I know." He lifted her hand in both of his. "You've got dirt in under your nails."

"I can live with that."

"Or I could lick it out." He met her eye and immediately slumped into a laugh. "Jesus, not a good thought. Not what I should have suggested. Not . . . suitable. I haven't known what to say for the whole of the time I've been here."

"You should have said." And she made sure to laugh immediately after and bring her other hand up to meet his. "I haven't, either."

"Tricky."

"Putting it mildly."

The breeze shifted, showed the silver under the leaves.

"I'm sorry, David. I made a mistake."

"Yeah. I made one, too."

They let their hands separate and began walking.

David brushed his clean knuckles down her arm, "I'll tell you something, though—I'm not especially good at this nature stuff, but I do think that we're going to have thunder, in fact I'm absolutely sure there'll be another storm tonight."

"It's possible. The leaves are turning."

"It's definite." He let a few more paces pass. "So we should stick together."

"For the night." She would kiss him soon.

Truly, no mistake.

And each one knowing the other was here, need opening to make them defenceless and bring them in, no harm done. "It might be wise. In case you decide to get frightened, or happy. Or whatever else." He tugged at a grass head as they strolled. "In case you decide."

"Which could happen at any time." The wood starting its

evening song, the sweet-shop scent of rhododendron strong beside them, the soft grumble of late bees, still working at the flowers, and David matching her, step for step, the best kind of wait between them and set to break. "At any time." And she allowed him: the way that he had been, that he would be soon, the way she would be with him: she permitted everything, made herself prepared.

"I know, love."

"Good. So that's all right, then. That's all right."

Acknowledgements

Versions of some of these stories have appeared in *New Writing 6* (Vintage), *Boston Review, Grand Street Magazine* and *Harlot Red* (Serpent's Tail), and have been broadcast on BBC Radio Four.

The author is grateful for time spent in Lewisboro, New York, as a guest of The Writers' Room.

A NOTE ABOUT THE AUTHOR

A. L. Kennedy lives in Glasgow. Her previous books include two collections of stories, four novels, and two works of nonfiction. She has received many prizes for her work, including the Somerset Maugham Award, the Encore Award, and the Saltire Scottish Book of the Year Award.

A NOTE ABOUT THE AUTHOR

A. L. Kennedy lives in Glasgow. Her previous books include two collections of stories, four novels, and two works of nonfiction. She has received many prizes for her work, including the Somerset Maugham Award, the Encore Award, and the Saltire Scottish Book of the Year Award.

A NOTE ON THE TYPE

This book was set in a modern adaptation of a type designed by the first William Caslon (1692–1766). The Caslon face, an artistic, easily read type, has enjoyed over two centuries of popularity in our own country. It is of interest to note that the first copies of the Declaration of Independence and the first paper currency distributed to the citizens of the newborn nation were printed in this typeface.

Composed by NK Graphics,
Keene, New Hampshire

Printed and bound by R. R. Donnelley & Sons,
Harrisonburg, Virginia

Designed by Soonyoung Kwon